THE STARS WITHIN

THE GIFT OF THE STARS BOOK 1

LENA ALISON KNIGHT

ONE

THIS WHOLE PLANET, Kerelle concluded, was a trashpile. She'd formed that hypothesis when reading through her mission briefing documents earlier in the week. The briefing hadn't used the word "trashpile," of course, but Kerelle had heard enough corporatespeak in her career to recognize what "small-output farm economy" and "low growth potential" were *really* saying. And, of course, there was the fact that SysTech had owned Elekar's mineral rights for decades, and had only decided to exercise them now that the colonists had stumbled across a rich cherium vein. The discovery of anything of value on Elekar had clearly surprised SysTech as much as anyone.

In the same vein, she suspected the "bandit insurgency" she was here to suppress was corporatespeak for "people who won't give us what we want." Not that it mattered - regardless of semantics, her orders were the same.

As the transport rumbled along and she gazed out at the rust-spattered scrubland speeding past, her initial opinion was confirmed. The stark landscape had been unappealing *before* the bombs and barbed wire, pollutant runoff from the mines had scarred the water and soil, and the sky had not budged from a sullen overcast beige since she arrived. If this was the world the Elekari had endured to find their cherium, Kerelle understood why they were fighting so hard to keep it.

The biggest question, really, was why SysTech had funded the initial colony at all. Clearly the company had had no idea the cherium was here, or they would have been voraciously strip-mining Elekar from the very start. Maybe initial surveys had overestimated the value of the more accessible mineral deposits; there certainly didn't seem to be anything else here that would merit corporate investment.

Regardless, they'd found something *now*, and the Elekari were trapped in the bargains their ancestors had made. If she thought about it too much, Kerelle would pity them, so she didn't think about it. Orders were orders and she could not disobey; having feelings about it all would only make things harder.

Ten years in the field had taught her that.

The passing vista slowed, the transport finally lurching to a teeth-rattling halt. A few moments later there was a tentative knock on her cabin door.

"Ma'am?" The young soldier saluted her as if she were an officer, keeping his eyes on the floor. His fear radiated at her senses. "Commander Nyra asked me to fetch you. We've arrived at HQ."

Kerelle smiled at him and nodded her acknowledgement. It had no effect on his discomfort. "Thank you, Private. I will meet the commander outside." He saluted again and ducked out of her cabin, his relief at leaving her presence bursting forth like a psychic beacon.

Once it would have bothered her that she terrified mundanes merely by proximity. At some point over the last decade, however, it had simply become part of life. Kerelle wasn't sure what that said about her - it was another thing she tried not to think about.

She gathered her small pack and made her way through the main body of the transport, serenely following the path hastily cleared for her by the disembarking soldiers. A scattered few, the veterans who had likely worked with the Psionic Corps before, simply held at stoic attention as she went by, and she gave them nods as she passed. From the others she got several salutes and several more nervous glances at the open-eye insignia on her jacket, and the slim alloy band at her throat.

Most of Kerelle's career had been spent embedded with SysTech's private military, the euphemistically-dubbed Security Force, and the scene had played out countless times over the last ten years. They were all on the same side here, of course, but that didn't mean the security troops weren't nervous at being near someone who could read their thoughts. Or set off explosions with her own. Nervous or not, she knew they'd appreciate her presence once they'd seen what she could do in the field.

Even if they still didn't want to sit too close to her in the mess.

COMMANDER NYRA WAS INDEED WAITING for Kerelle at the mouth of the transport. Nyra was a lifer in SysTech's private military, and she looked the part, from her close-cropped iron hair to her perpetually stern expression. The commander was a no-nonsense woman without much patience for flights of fancy, and she'd never seemed overly bothered by PsiCorp agents. Kerelle rather liked her.

True to form, the older woman wasted no time. "You're getting an official welcome, Agent." Nyra told her briskly. "Governor wants you escorted to his mansion straight away."

Kerelle suppressed a sigh. The last thing she wanted to do after the long trip here was make nice with whatever bureaucrat with delusions of grandeur had been assigned to rein in the wayward colony. But duty called, as it frequently did, and so she pasted on a pleasant expression and stepped down into Elekar's dusty soil.

She followed Nyra past a series of squat, cube-shaped structures, most cheaply constructed from plastic siding and metal frames. The headquarters compound had obviously been a village not too far in the past, its houses and barns now converted to barracks and supply stores. Some still held small personal touches that the occupying force hadn't yet bothered to remove. All were coated in the greyish dust that seemed to be Elekar's signature feature, and which was doubtlessly already beginning to coat Kerelle too.

SysTech troops swarmed the area like grey-clad ants, moving supplies, running drills and raising fortifications around the perimeter. A handful of Elekari hovered about at the edges, silent and grim. Kerelle wondered if they were the village's former inhabitants, and where they were shuffled off to when SysTech commandeered their houses.

She wouldn't have been at all surprised if they'd been simply thrown out to fend for themselves.

Nyra came to a halt outside the largest structure and saluted. Two men were waiting at the doors. Presumably, the taller man on the left was the one she was here to see - she doubted anyone but the new SysTech governor would be wearing an expensive suit out here. The dour-faced older man beside him was more of a mystery, but his simple clothing suggested he was a local.

Fancy Suit gave her an oily smile as she approached.

"Agent Evandra, I presume?" The taller man spread his arms as if to encompass the scrubland, the bustling soldiers and the squat concrete building behind him. "Governor Bhasel Yalar Helneres, lately arrived from regional headquarters. Welcome to Elekar, my dear, I'm so very pleased you were able to come."

Kerelle responded with an appropriate platitude, maintaining the polite fiction she'd had any choice in the matter. The other man said nothing, giving her the barest nod of acknowledgement. Almost *definitely* a local. Helneres ignored him and kept going.

"I'm sure they filled you in on the situation here, but these bandits have been getting more and more bold. I wasn't sure the Tallimau office was taking things seriously, but it's good to see my concerns were misplaced." He swept a hand up as if to wave off his earlier misgivings, conveniently drawing attention to the metal circlet resting on his temples. She doubted it was accidental.

Kerelle kept her face pleasantly neutral. Psiblocker circlets, capable of negating telepathy and significantly dampening the effects of telekinesis, were undeniably a status symbol. They were rare, expensive, and one of the most coveted perks of corporate senior management. The particular psiblocker Helneres was wearing, however, was not particularly high quality, and she suspected he had purchased it himself.

Rather *less* of a status symbol, then. A corporate-issued psiblocker indicated someone was important enough that the company was willing to spend a small fortune to protect them from psionic incursion; a private purchase merely indicated someone had a small fortune to spend. She wondered if Helneres knew how little value that small fortune had gotten him.

Oh, it would probably work fine against a class-1 telepath, so she supposed it was helpful if he was paranoid about his secretary reading his mind. For a class-3 telepath like Kerelle, however, it barely counted as an impediment to accessing his thoughts.

Fortunately for Helneres, she really didn't give a damn what he was thinking anyway.

He was looking at her like he expected her to be impressed,

and Kerelle supposed she ought to make some sort of interested noise. But it had been a very long trip, Helneres was currently making it longer, and frankly she just didn't want to give him the satisfaction. Her orders were to assist Helneres and the SysTech Security Force in putting down the rebellion; she wasn't obligated to also kiss his ass. She just smiled politely.

The nonplussed discomfort flicked across his face in an instant and was gone, his oily demeanor once again in place.

"Do come in, you've had quite the journey and we have much to discuss. Karek will have the staff bring tea; not up to Tallimau standards, I'm afraid, but it's usually drinkable. His people try their best." This time his dismissive gesture included the silent local man. Karek's stoic frown did not change, though Kerelle thought she detected a slight tightening of his jaw at being relegated to butler.

Elekar had been self-governing, before SysTech invoked the clause in the colony's charter that allowed it to assume direct control. Based on his presence in the welcome party and apparent working relationship with the governor, she was going to take a shot in the dark that Karek had been the one in charge here prior to Helneres's arrival. Kerelle wondered if the newly-designated Governor's Mansion had been his house.

A short time later she was seated in a small receiving room, simply furnished but clean. Helneres made some tut-tutting noises about their rustic surroundings, and finally got down to business.

"This bandit insurgency has been a thorn in my side since I arrived. Thanks to their sabotage and interference, we're at least six months behind schedule on the cherium extraction. And even the law-abiding locals have been worse than useless. I've had to suspend mining operations altogether at one of the most promising sites until we can import offworld labor, so many of them were refusing to show up for work."

Karek's gruff voice cut in for the first time. "There were three attacks on the Danbem site. A lot of good people died." Helneres rolled his eyes. "Losses were well within acceptable margins, given the current price of cherium. The money we're losing from stopped production far outstrips the cost of paying out death compensation for fifty-odd miners."

"Fifty-seven," Karek corrected quietly. Helneres ignored him. "For a bunch of poorly trained farmers, the bandits have proved surprisingly tenacious. They strike out of nowhere, then vanish back into whatever dens and warrens they crouch in to wait for us. Our troops are stuck in the mud."

"They won't give a step if they don't have to," Karek answered roughly. Helneres looked peeved at the interjection. "They know the land, and they're defending their homes."

"Homes their great-grandparents built with SysTech funding," Helneres snapped. "The colony's founding contracts clearly designate SysTech as sole legal owner of any mineral resources, your people simply don't want to pay the terms of your debt. I have no sympathy for freeloaders who try to renege on their contracts."

He looked to Kerelle as if for support. She wasn't inclined to give it; for a moment, her collar felt heavy at her throat. She was quite familiar with one-sided SysTech "contracts."

Instead, she tried to move things along. "I assume there is a plan of action."

"Of course, agent. I apologize for all the interruptions. Karek here was the Elekari headman until we were forced to take a firmer hand in managing our interests, and sometimes he forgets that his laxity with this world's riffraff is what got us into this situation." Karek's stoic glower did not change, though Kerelle could sense the fury simmering beneath his skin. "As I was saying, our troops have been stuck in the mud while the bandits run riot. A little PsiCorp firepower ought to tilt the odds, eh?"

So it was that the next day found her heading out with Commander Nyra's unit to a nearby village accused of providing aid to the "bandits." It had no strategic value, but Helneres made it clear that the village itself wasn't what he was after.

"Rip it apart," he'd instructed her, a distastefully gleeful note in his voice. "Let them see what they're dealing with now. Let them see the cost of resistance."

NYRA CALLED the halt at the edge of a field. Low clusters of hardy-looking leaves surrounded them, planted in neat rows that the soldiers were currently trampling. From across the dusty field they could see the village itself, a ramshackle collection of corrugated-metal huts. Like the new "capital" she'd landed in, the village had clearly been built on the cheap.

Nyra made a sign with her hand, and the unit fanned out around her and Kerelle in a loose formation that could easily tighten up in a protective wall if needed. It wouldn't be.

"Listen up, you lot. This is a demonstration, not a massacre. On my signal deploy the flashes to roust them, and Agent Evandra will take it from there. Defensive tactics if attacked, but no live weapons otherwise. Dead people don't talk and we want this story spread far and wide."

Nyra turned her attention to Kerelle.

"We'll lead with the flashscreens, Agent. After that it's up to you." Kerelle gave her a single nod and took a few steps forward to get better line of sight.

An uneasy knot of villagers was beginning to form in the central square, seemingly unsure if they were better served ignoring the SysTech soldiers' presence or watching their every move. They really *ought* to be running.

A familiar sick feeling coiled in her gut at what was about to happen, at what she was about to do. Kerelle shoved it down, trying to find the detachment she'd felt on the transport. How she felt about this, or anything, didn't matter; it was better to just not feel at all. She took a steadying breath and readied herself.

A blinding flash, then another as the flashscreen grenades hit. The villagers began to shout in alarm, scattering across the square. Time to do her part.

Kerelle scanned targets quickly and selected a building on the outskirts - it looked like it was probably a barn or a storage structure, and it was less likely to be occupied. She gave it a quick telepathic scan anyway, confirming that it was empty. It was, and so she wrapped her power around it and *yanked*.

The metal shrieked in protest as it was rent apart, the pieces scattering violently around it to barrel into other structures or erupt in clouds of grey dust against the ground. She grabbed another building and dealt it the same fate as a cacophony of screams rose, the villagers beginning to panic.

PsiCorp. The PsiCorp was here.

She flung some rubble around for effect, then started on another hut. Kerelle preferred efficiency in her destruction, but the whole point here was the show. It was working, too - the villagers' terror burned like wildfire against her senses. The more sensible ones were fleeing in the opposite direction, but others were transfixed by the spectacle of disaster visited upon them. Kerelle bit back a groan of frustration.

Run, you idiots! RUN! She had never excelled at the subtle art of telepathically planting ideas in others' heads, but there was nothing remotely subtle in this situation anyway. She hit the remaining villagers with a wave of psionic suggestion, immediately rewarded as most of them obeyed the sudden overwhelming urge to scatter. When she brought down a shockwave that sent the remaining structures toppling, the village was virtually emptied.

Sudden silence descended, all eyes on the billowing dust

clouds above the small, sad scrap heaps that had been these people's homes and livelihoods. She hoped the villagers themselves had all escaped with their lives.

Kerelle turned away. "We're done here, Commander."

"I see that, Agent," Nyra responded. Her voice was even, but Kerelle could sense her unease. Nyra had worked with PsiCorp before and was probably familiar with telekinetic destruction, but very few PsiCorp could match Kerelle for scale. Telekinetics strong enough to be ranked Class-3 were not common, and as their group took in the scene Kerelle couldn't help but think that was probably for the best.

She started back towards their transport. The soldiers gave her wide berth.

TWO

ROCKS CRUNCHED underfoot as their column trudged through the dry lake. At least, Kerelle assumed it had been a lake once; now it was little more than a wide, shallow pit coated in gravel and, naturally, grey dust.

A pebble worked its way into her boot, and she shook her foot to try to dislodge it without breaking stride. The lakebed was a pain in the ass to walk through, but she understood why they were doing it. One only had to look at the column of marching soldiers and count how fewer there were than five months prior.

She'd been on Elekar for five months, though it often felt like longer. It was four months since they'd left the relative comfort of the capital; it was three months, one week since Elekari resistance members had infiltrated the maintenance crew and planted the charges that left dozens dead and made smouldering wrecks of their primary transports. The bulk of the SysTech force had been on foot since.

Kind of a metaphor for this whole campaign, really. Over her career Kerelle had been included in a number of military actions that had not gone smoothly, but even by the standard of past shitty experiences Elekar was in a class of its own.

The SysTech soldiers might have been better trained and armed, but as Karek had predicted the Elekari knew the land, and how to use it to their advantage. True, SysTech had made considerable progress against the rebels, and true they held significantly more secured territory than five months prior. But the rebels were every bit as tenacious as Helneres had claimed, and quite a bit more numerous than he let on. Guerilla action had inflicted terrible casualties on the SysTech force - and their supplies. Food and medicine were both running alarmingly low.

The broad, flat expanse of the lake offered no cover in any direction, and made the kind of lightning stealth attacks favored by the Elekari unfeasible. When you looked at it that way, this stupid dead lake was the safest place they'd been in weeks.

Up ahead the column was called to a halt, and word soon spread back that they were stopping to make camp. Kerelle's aching feet cheered, even as her back groaned at the prospect of sleeping on a pile of tiny rocks. Her rumbling stomach, too, was unlikely to be fully appeased with their increasingly-tight rations, but at least she'd be able to eat *something*.

The tents went up with the quick efficiency of long practice, and soon the camp was awash with clanks and chatter. Kerelle found an out-of-the-way spot and sat herself down, sipping from her canteen as she watched the camp bustle about its business. She wished it were tea instead of water - or better yet, whiskey - but after yet another long day on the march, even lukewarm canteen water seemed satisfying. The important part was that she was off her feet.

The soldiers nearest her sitting spot shot her wary glances, but carried on with what they were doing. They were still uncomfortable with her presence, and if past experiences were a guide they always would be. But the outright fear she'd encountered on arrival had faded under the weight of familiarity. Some time around eight weeks of eating the same shitty food, sleeping in the same shitty tents, and marching through the same shitty landscape, Kerelle had shed some mystique.

All the same, she upped her telepathic shields to avoid picking up any stray thoughts or feelings. She could see they were uncomfortable with her proximity; she didn't need that discomfort leaking into her head.

Telepathic noise taken care of, Kerelle leaned back against the side of her tent, shifting into some approximation of a comfortable position. She was just contemplating a nap when a voice at her elbow broke through.

"Agent Evandra? Er, ma'am?"

Kerelle eased an eye open and nodded at the lieutenant. The young woman straightened and continued. "Ma'am, the commander requests your presence at a meeting. His tent in fifteen minutes please, ma'am."

That sounded like the *last* thing she wanted to do right now, but it wasn't the lieutenant's fault, so Kerelle thanked her with a smile even as she inwardly groaned and clambered to her feet.

Commander Zereyl's tent was the largest, in the center of the camp. There was a familiar pang of sadness in her chest as she approached the tent; it had been Nyra's, before a well-aimed grenade thrown from the cover of nearby crags. She and Nyra hadn't been *friends*, exactly, but Kerelle had liked her and regretted her loss. Commander Zereyl was professional and good at his job, but noticeably less comfortable with PsiCorp.

Or maybe just PsiCorp who could rip whole villages apart.

She found most of the officers assembled already. The SysTech force were all professionals, and everyone in the tent waited with polite expressions, but she could see the strain at the edges of their faces. A sort of resigned dread hovered over the assembly, as everyone braced for the latest disaster. To Kerelle's surprise and theirs, it was rather the opposite.

Zereyl got straight to business. "As you know we've been

heading this direction with the goal of taking Albant," he announced, referring to the largest settlement in the area. "I've just received word that Albant's governing council has disavowed the bandits and officially declared its intent to cooperate with SysTech authorities." Murmurs arose from the crowded tent, and died when he raised his voice to continue.

"I've also been informed that Corporate will be sending reinforcements to expedite the campaign. At first light we head for Albant, where we'll fortify until additional supplies and personnel arrive."

For the first time in weeks, something like hope threaded through the tent.

———

THE BURST of human thoughts ahead lit up in her awareness. Kerelle pulled up short and signaled to Commander Zereyl to call a halt. He did, several hands tightening on weapons as they watched her for an indication. More than once on this march, Kerelle's open senses had kept them from walking into an ambush.

She stretched her senses outward, scanning for more of the minds she'd sensed. It could just be a group of foragers or a camp of refugees, but she doubted it. Not all the way out here, not at the mouth of a canyon that practically screamed "ambush site." If the rebels knew Albant had surrendered - and she had to assume they did - then they also knew the SysTech force would have to pass through here on their way to claim it. In their shoes, *she'd* set an ambush here.

There - she caught the loudest thoughts and held them. A jumble of nervous impatience, fear, savage anticipation. Tense waiting for the signal, to stream forward for the attack once the corporate bastards hit the mines. *See what those fancy uniforms are good for then. Except they've stopped, shit, shit, they have the* witch *with them, she knows something is up, have to go now and try to push them into the minefield -*

Kerelle snapped back to herself with barely enough time to shout a warning about the mines before the first shots started landing around them. A few of the SysTech troops dodged the wrong way anyway, and explosions and screams blotted out any other noise. Kerelle shut it out to concentrate; there was nothing she could do for them now.

Zereyl shouted orders around her, trying to get the unit regrouped. The rebels were perched on the lips of the canyon, firing as fast as their antiquated rifles could get off the shots. Kerelle threw up a shield of telekinetic force to deflect and most of the bullets pinged harmlessly to ground, though a few cries of pain behind her meant she hadn't been fast enough.

Still, the relative reprieve gave the SysTech squad the seconds they needed to scramble back into position, and get their guns up. At Zereyl's signal she dropped the shield, and the battle began in earnest.

The rebel group was unusually large, and they held the superior position, using it mercilessly to shower the SysTech team with shots. But the corporate soldiers were better armed, with better long-range accuracy, and they began picking off the rebels along the edge.

She'd *had* to drop the shield around their force; it would deflect the enemy's bullets, but also stop their own. Her own weapons, however, had no such limitations. Kerelle kept up a tight telekinetic shield around herself as she quickly scanned for targets - and fortunately so. By the steady rain of bullets against her shields, a number of the Elekari were specifically aiming for *her*.

Between the number of combatants and the smoke from the mines, it was hard to zero in on her assailants' location. Kerelle tried to focus on the direction the bullets were coming from - there, up and left. She flung a hard bolt of energy into the general area, and was rewarded when one of the rebels shrieked and toppled over the canyon's edge.

It also gave her an idea.

Kerelle caught Zereyl's eye and gestured sharply downward. He caught on immediately and nodded his agreement, raising his voice to be heard over the din as he shouted the orders to move back. Slowly the SysTech group retreated back. Her shot was clear.

Kerelle threw her power in an violent shove against the canyon wall. The telekinetic blow she delivered shook the entire cliffside, sending a few attackers hurtling over the edge. Another hit and she had her objective - the canyon wall collapsed, bringing most of the rebels down with it. She caught the boulders as they came down, turning their momentum to fling them upwards at the other side of the canyon. The falling rebels she left to fall - the soldiers could finish off those that survived. The remaining group erupted into a chaotic retreat.

When it was over, they were left with the groaning wounded and far too many bodies. The mines had wreaked a terrible toll on those who had been too close, and the ambush had claimed many others. She'd done everything she could to protect the squad, but still Kerelle felt a thin curl of guilt as she watched them regroup. As always, it hadn't been enough.

The surviving SysTech squad grimly began gathering up their fallen comrades and preparing the wounded for transport. The question of whether their depleted medical resources could even do anything to help them remained unspoken. Albant was still days away, and there was little reason to be optimistic of the facilities they'd find there. The best medical technology on Elekar was likely whatever scraps they had left in their supply packs.

Still, they carried out their tasks with bleak efficiency. They had done this far too many times over the past few months.

LIKE THE OTHER towns she'd seen on Elekar, Albant had been cheaply constructed long before any of its current residents were born. Drab and worn down, its blocked-concrete architecture had likely been bleakly utilitarian even before years of hard use had worn away any artistry.

Still, Kerelle's heart lifted as she crested the hill to look down on those stark blocks, interlaced with paved streets and hosting presumably-functional electrical and sanitation systems. Real beds, running water, and meals that didn't come out of a can.

Five months on campaign had a way of adjusting one's concept of luxury.

The SysTech force approached Albant with caution, though the gates had been thrown wide open in anticipation of their arrival. That was to be expected in the settlement's surrender, but they'd learned the hard way over the prior months that Elekari hospitality was not always what it seemed. Faking the surrender of a major settlement to facilitate an ambush or assassination was *probably* beyond the rebels' means, but their foes had proven nothing if not creative.

Kerelle sent her senses forward as they drew closer, questing for any ill intent. There was a morass of thoughts and feelings projecting from inside - sorrow, anxiety, an almost smothering dread. Mingled with it all was a sort of bleak resignation to SysTech's inevitability. No one was happy about it, but the surrender in Albant was genuine.

Satisfied that were no hidden assailants waiting to lob carnage into their midst, Kerelle gave Zereyl a small nod. He signalled to the troops behind them, and SysTech advanced into Albant.

Most of the concrete buildings were tightly shuttered as they passed, with only a few curious faces craning out of open windows. The majority of Albant's residents had apparently concluded that staying out of sight was their safest option. Kerelle couldn't blame them.

The town square came into view, with Albant's council assembled to formally offer the settlement's allegiance. From the emotional projections that brushed Kerelle's senses, they wished *they* could have stayed out of sight as well.

The lead councilor nonetheless pasted on a smile at their approach.

"Welcome to our humble village," he declared in a voice pitched to carry. "We in Albant are honored to host our esteemed partners from SysTech, and reaffirm our commitment to upholding Elekar's charter." His smiled widened at that last part, as though to counter the recency of Albant's collaborationist conversion with sheer enthusiasm.

The next half-hour passed with the special tedium of important functions. Papers were signed, formal declarations were made, applause duly offered. Kerelle might not like Commander Zereyl quite as much as she'd liked Nyra, but credit where it was due, he was a consummate professional. Zereyl was taciturn but gracious in accepting Albant's capitulation, and even listened politely as the lead councilor launched into a rather transparent speech about cooperation and new futures.

Kerelle kept her face set in the pleasantly neutral expression she'd cultivated over the years, but her mind wandered. She had no illusions about why Zereyl had asked her to accompany him and the other senior officers to accept the town's surrender - it was the same reason she'd swept her hair up in a messy bun to ensure the PsiCorp insignia on her jacket was clearly visible. She was here to listen politely, provide security against unpleasant surprises, and not-so-subtly remind the councilors why they were surrendering.

At this point Kerelle was reasonably certain everything was above board, but she gave the councilors a quick telepathic scan anyway for the sake of due diligence. She only had to brush their surface thoughts to see that such caution was unwarranted.

The group was putting on a decent show of enthusiasm, but fear and anxiety bubbled thick on their minds, along with a steady mix of guilt. This wasn't what anyone wanted, but they'd heard the stories and seen the pictures from the north. SysTech was going to win this eventually, by sheer numbers if nothing else, and there was no point in throwing all their people's lives away. Hopefully SysTech would appreciate their peaceful acquiescence, and Albant wouldn't suffer in the occupation.

Kerelle hoped that worked out for them. She'd never known SysTech to be appreciative.

Her attention snapped back to the welcome party as the lead councilor's cadence changed. He'd finally wrapped up his speech and moved on to practical matters. He and Zereyl were discussing something about quartering the officers in the councilors' own homes as a gesture of good faith. Apparently they'd already drawn up a list.

"Lady Agent?" One of the councilors stepped towards her, offering her a bright smile betrayed by his trembling hands. "Olan Merus Dalsen, Third Councilor for Albant. It will be my honor to be your host during your stay here."

Running water and real beds, indeed.

HER PACK WAS NOT LARGE, but Councilor Dalsen insisted on having it carried for her to his residence, and on personally introducing her to her family and staff. Guilt bloomed in her gut at their obvious terror at finding the PsiCorp in their midst. The pale, trembling lady of the house managed a wan smile and whispered welcome, one sobbing child in her arms and another hiding behind her legs, while Dalsen's effusive assurance that she was an honored guest began to take on a tinge of desperation. When the door to her quarters finally closed behind her, it was not a moment too soon.

It was a sumptuous suite, by Elekar standards - enough so that she wondered if Dalsen had given her his own rooms. The furniture looked like it had been purchased within the last decade, with all the linens in good repair. A small bowl of native fruits had been left invitingly on the sitting table. The interior walls had even been painted a soft ivory, lending the room a domestic warmth that many of Elekar's structures markedly lacked.

Then her eyes fell on a corner of the lavatory, and Kerelle couldn't help a squeal of delight. A bathtub. *A real bathtub.*

All her guilt at displacing the councilor's family evaporated like the curling steam as she settled into the hot, buoyant water. She leaned her head back and let it soak into her scalp, the tension of five months of camping beginning to loosen in her back. There were probably reports she should be writing or dignitaries she should be meeting somewhere, but flaming stars, this was the best she'd felt in months. She was going to *enjoy* it.

Kerelle lingered in the bathtub until the water grew tepid, and it was no longer possible to ignore the greyish tinge it had taken on. She probably should have rinsed off *before* getting in the tub, she thought ruefully, and settled for a decadently long shower with indulgent use of the scented cleansing gels she found inside. She stepped out feeling like herself again, for the first time in months.

The chamber's large mirror confirmed that she *looked* like herself again too, her hair hanging smooth and jet black instead of ragged dust-grey. Kerelle had never been particularly preoccupied with her appearance, but she couldn't deny that it felt good to recognize her own reflection.

Immediate needs satisfied, she grabbed her battered tablet and one of the fruits, and padded over to the bed. Along with regular bathing, real food, and comfortable beds, months on the trail had deprived her of regular datanet access. Sure a family as well-to-do as this one appeared to be would have a reliable connection.

They did, and once her messages loaded in, she instantly regretted not checking them immediately.

Agent Evandra,

I hope this message finds you well. My most recent project closed last week, and I've been informed this morning that I will be joining you on Elekar to assist in the next phase of the campaign. Logistics are still being finalized, but I should be underway within a week. I look forward to working with you again.

Best,

Galhen Tarau Ambrel

Senior Agent, C3 TLP, C3 REG

Kerelle leaned back into the pillows, unable to keep the giddy grin off her face. It was an impeccably professional message, of course, nothing that would raise any eyebrows, but there was meaning there for *her* that a corporate inspector wouldn't see. The most exciting part was that he would be *here*, of course, but his references to the timeline were significant as well. When she left for Elekar, Galhen was assigned to a project on one of the Baleal Ring stations. If he'd departed Baleal for Elekar when he'd planned to, that mean he might already be back in range.

She fired off a quick response.

Agent Ambrel,

Apologies for the delayed response, I've been in the field without reliable datanet access. Glad to hear of your new assignment - your assistance

on the Elekar campaign will be very valuable. I will give you an updated
briefing on the status of the mission when you arrive. Safe travels.

Best,

Kerelle Evandra

Senior Agent, C3 TLP, C3 TLK

There, nothing scandalous in that.

It wasn't that serious relationships between PsiCorp agents
were *forbidden*, exactly. Certainly not. If she'd asked a PsiCorp
division manager if her relationship with Galhen were *allowed*,
they assuredly wouldn't say *no*.

But they would talk instead about *duty*, and *priorities*, and
how important it was to make sure that the work came first.
And how they might certainly become *concerned*, if they felt a
pair of agents might allow personal considerations to affect their
performance.

Short flings between PsiCorp agents were hardly problematic
- they were rather encouraged, even. Longer-term entangle-
ments, however, had the potential to become *concerning* to
management. Kerelle suspected the real reason was that SysTech
didn't like its PsiCorp forgetting who owned them.

The Tallimau office's PsiCorp director was likely aware that
two of his vaunted double-class-3 agents slept together when-
ever they managed to share leave, and he might well be mildly
concerned. If he'd known that the sex was the least of it, that
they'd shared a bond of support and affection since they'd met
as teens in the training academy over a decade prior, he would
be highly *concerned*.

And if he'd known that they had stumbled upon an apparently unique ability to visit each other in dreams, and concealed
that ability most of their lives, well. Then he would be apoplec-
tically *concerned*.

Kerelle and Galhen took special care to stay conscientious in
their work, so that any existing *concern* might be minimized. As

for the rest, well, it was not so difficult for two top-ranked telepaths to be discreet.

The dreaming had kept them close through years of frequent physical separation, but like all telepathy it had limits of distance. Through the years, however, she and Galhen had discovered that their range with each other was quite considerable - as long as they were in the same star system, the dreaming would usually work. The ship carrying him to Elekar might already be close enough to try. And now he knew *she* was in range as well.

Kerelle fell asleep smiling.

THREE

HER CONSCIOUSNESS SHIFTED. It could have been minutes or hours later, time was never clear in the dream. The world simply came into focus, and she was somewhere else.

The sky above her was a lush canopy of violet, soft stars beginning to emerge from its folds. She was lying on warm sand, and nearby she heard the gentle crash of waves. She sat up to a view of a sparkling sea gilded orange by the setting sun, bright flowers hugging the edges of the beach. Kerelle recognized her surroundings - an island resort they had once visited together.

Smiling, she turned to Galhen sitting beside her.

"Nostalgic for Aulayie?" She asked it teasingly as she leaned her lips to his.

"I thought you could probably use a bit of paradise," he responded with a smile. His kiss was warm and welcoming, and almost as good as the real thing. He exhaled against her cheek. "I've missed you."

She buried her face in his shoulder, and for a moment they simply held each other. It had been months. Finally she shifted to lean her head against him, and they stared out at the ersatz ocean together. Even knowing it wasn't real, the feel of his arms around her lent her peace.

"Did things go well at Baleal?" she asked finally. She didn't want to talk about Elekar, not yet.

"As well as it could. I was able to save a fair number of the victims, and we determined the virus wasn't anything intentionally introduced. The other C3 telepath I was paired with had an espionage background, and while I worked on eliminating the virus she was fantastic at finding out what actually *did* happen. Which, for the record, was someone in a bioresearch lab fumbling their safety protocol and tracking the damn thing outside."

She shivered a bit. "I don't like that you were that close to some kind of supervirus."

He gave her a half-smile. "Kerelle, you know perfectly well that in an epidemic, wherever I am is the safest place to be." It was simple truth. Besides his telepathy, Galhen was a regenerative - that rare kind of psionic people were actually *happy* to encounter.

"I know. I worry anyway." She cuddled in closer and twined her fingers through his soft hair. "And they're sending you straight from that to Elekar."

His voice was quiet. "I was briefed, but you know how that goes. How are things *actually?*"

She laughed bitterly. "They're bad. Worst I've seen in years. What did your briefing say?"

"Well-entrenched, well-organized bandits wreaking havoc on planetary stability, dark hints that they're armed and funded by Consolidated Energy to undermine our operations and manipulate cherium prices."

Kerelle stared open-mouthed. "*ConEn? That's* what they're trying to make this out as?

"That's what the documents said, so I have to assume that's the narrative they'll be pushing to the public." He gave her another half-smile, this one with a sardonic tinge. "I rather expected you might have a different version of events."

"Elekar is in *civil war*, Galhen. Half the population hates us and is fighting tooth and nail to keep the cherium, the other half also hates us but doesn't think it's worth dying for. There's no corporate chess here, just a bunch of desperate people trying to hold on to what little they have." She sighed in disgust. "'*Armed by ConEn,*' stars above. Their rifles are as old as we are. The only reason they're able to fight us at all is that they're smart enough not to do it head on."

She flopped back on the sand, staring up at the dusky sky. "I almost wish it *were* true about ConEn. I don't feel as awful about it when we're fighting people who chose this."

He leaned down and ran a deliberate finger across her collar. "We never chose this either," he reminded her. His own collar glinted in the golden light.

"I know," she sighed. "And I know there's nothing I can do differently. But after five months helping beat down impover- ished farmers it's hard to look myself in the face."

He gave her a soft kiss against her jaw and drew her back into his arms. "What else can you do? Refuse your orders and wait for the Director to activate your collar for defiance? Let them torture you until you agree to do it anyway, or kill you if you won't obey? They'll have a replacement telekinetic landed in weeks. Your death won't save anyone on Elekar."

He murmured it gently, and they both knew it was true. It had been true from the moment that company representatives had knocked on their parents' doors more than twenty years ago, armed with the legal right to conscript any psionic children in SysTech territory. Kerelle didn't remember much from her life before the PsiCorp - perhaps her family had fought a futile battle to keep her. Galhen's parents hadn't even tried.

"I can't even help *our* people," she confessed. "I can try to spot ambushes and stop attackers, but it hasn't been enough.

We've lost far too many to the rebels' traps." She rolled over to meet his vivid green eyes. "Is that why they're sending you?"

"It is. They're sending several of us, actually, including some backup for you. The company very much wants this ended soon, and our superiors are well aware that your assistance is the only thing keeping the advance going. But yes, for my part I'm to take over leading the medical team, and obviously do what I can in the field."

Kerelle nodded silently. It was something, at least, to have fewer of the Security Force leaving Elekar in body bags.

Some of her bleak thoughts must have leaked into the dream, for he sent her feelings of soft warmth and drew her in to nestle closer against him.

"I'm sorry, darling," he whispered against her hair. "But we'll get through it, just like always."

Kerelle offered a weary nod of agreement. Elekar wasn't her first distasteful mission, and it wouldn't be the last.

IN THE DAYS THAT FOLLOWED, Albant became a frenzy of activity. News of the impending reinforcements spread quickly through the troops, and with it a marked increase in morale. Albant had provided more comfortable sleeping quarters than the open fields, but the town's meager stores of food and medicine had offered little improvement from their field rations. Knowing that they would soon receive more troops - and more supplies - lifted spirits considerably, and the SysTech force approached the necessary preparations with renewed vigor.

And there were many preparations to be made. Elekar's only spaceport was back in the capital, but reinforcements would be flown to Albant on air shuttles. Those shuttles needed somewhere to land. With the tight-lipped acquiescence of the council, the surrounding fields were harvested early and converted to makeshift landing pads, and any space that could be was cleared to accommodate the new arrivals.

A week after they arrived in Albant, the first air shuttle made its dusty descent onto the new landing strip. The entire force stopped to cheer.

Another soon followed, and another. The skies were soon thick with SysTech vessels ferrying troops and supplies, and the buzz of air shuttle engines faded into a constant feature of Albant's environs. The dust clouds they kicked up were considerable as well, but as she tore into the first full ration she'd eaten in months, Kerelle fervently concluded it was worth it. She doubted anyone on the Security Force would disagree.

Even all the way from the capital, Kerelle sensed it the moment Galhen's ship touched down. His presence lit up her senses like a beacon as their psionic bond flared to life, bringing with it a soft and constant awareness of his mood and wellbeing. When they were close enough like this, Kerelle was never really alone. She sent him a telepathic pulse of joy and affection, barely suppressing a grin as he returned the feelings.

You're a bit more cheerful than when we spoke last, he observed.

A full stomach is rather buoying feeling, darling, even when it's full of standard rations. If you ever want to feel appreciative for a packet of rehydrated vegetable protein, try going to bed hungry for weeks beforehand.

I'll keep that in mind as we eat rehydrated vegetable protein for the forseeable future. The response was overlaid with sympathy, and relief that things had improved. *There's another few crates of it scheduled to fly in with me.*

Ah, that was a subject more exciting then rations. *When does your shuttle arrive in Albant?*

Late afternoon. We've got to make it through an official welcome tea with the governor first.

Lucky you. Have you met Helneres in person yet?

He shared a burst of imagery in response. Helneres held court from an ornate couch that bordered on ostentatious, particularly in the context of the rest of Elekar. A small group of young PsiCorp were seated in a half-circle around him. He was primarily speaking to Galhen, of course, as the senior agent, but would sometimes condescend to address the younger psionics as well. Mostly he simply expounded on his views of Elekar, the Elekari, and the excellent work he was bringing about. Knowing the junior agents would take their cues from him, Galhen kept his features carefully schooled in bland politeness and nodded at the appropriate places.

Oh, that looks delightful, *darling. I'm so sorry to be missing it. He's redecorated since I was there a few months ago. I would have remembered that couch.*

I fear I'll never be able to forget it. By the way, when you told me he was a self-important asshole, I think you were being overly diplomatic.

Kerelle laughed aloud, drawing startled glances from a pair of nearby workers. She felt better already.

GALHEN'S GROUP survived their tea with Helneres, and their shuttle finally cruised into Albant as the sun tilted toward the horizon. Kerelle joined Zereyl and his senior staff as they met the PsiCorp shuttle at the landing pad. Galhen's eyes glinted as he gave her a perfectly professional greeting, and an enthused telepathic embrace. A few smiling handshakes later he was off to the field hospital. A true reunion, alas, would have to wait; for now there was work to do.

"Senior Agent Evandra?" Speaking of work. Kerelle's attention snapped back to the two young PsiCorp agents who had followed Galhen down from the shuttle - presumably the telekinetics she'd been told to expect. She recognized them from Galhen's memory of the tea session.

"Agent Alna Marsel Rainav, class-2 telekinetic. Reporting from the Uliste office, ma'am," the young woman announced, saluting smartly. "This is Agent Selon Faremil Kalnarr, class-2 telekinetic also."

"Shield specialist, ma'am." Selon's murmured addendum was barely audible. He seemed to be the shy one, though she had no doubt he was good at his job. Kerelle offered what she hoped was a reassuring smile.

"Welcome to Elekar. I assume you were briefed on the situation here?"

"Yes ma'am. We were advised that the bandits have been driven back from the primary mining centers but still pose a threat to outlying areas, and have proved capable of inflicting high casualties on a superior force. We are to report in to you and provide assistance in suppressing the rogue element and assuring the security of SysTech mining operations."

Alna's breathless recitation carried an eager undertone, as though she were hoping to be awarded a gold star for excellent memorization. Kerelle's private estimate of their ages shifted downward. "And ma'am...ma'am I would just like to say that it is an honor to serve with you and we are happy to be able to help."

The nervous energy clicked into place. They'd never met a class 3 telekinetic. Well, that wasn't too surprising. C3 TLK weren't a numerous bunch, and even within the PsiCorp the C3 capacity for destruction lent a certain...distinction.

"I'm pleased to meet you both as well." Kerelle kept her voice smooth and professional. She needed these two to have their heads in the game once they got back on the march. "You're correct that our enemy has proven difficult to eliminate. Our forces have been stationed here to regroup for several weeks, but once the additional troops and supplies are all here we'll move out."

"Do you know where we're headed, ma'am?"

"Intel believes the rebels are concentrated in the east. You probably heard they rely on guerilla tactics - we'll need to flush

them out. I saw in your records you both have live combat experience?" They nodded, and she gave them a once-over. Neither had had a *lot* of combat experience, and she would have preferred more seasoned reinforcements, but at least neither was going to faint at the sight of blood.

"See the quartermaster for your housing assignments, then you're at liberty for the night. I advise you to take advantage of being here in town - it will probably be months before you sleep in a bed this comfortable again."

A brief flicker of dismay crossed both their faces, but to their credit the two C2s just nodded their understanding. As they headed off to sort out their lodging, Kerelle decided to follow her own advice and indulge in an long bath in her borrowed quarters' glorious tub. Galhen had muted their bond shortly after he left, which meant he was busy and needed to concentrate. He would contact her when he was able to.

Until then, she might as well luxuriate in bubbles.

FOUR

LATE IN THE EVENING, she felt Galhen's light touch on her mind. *I've finished up at the hospital. Are you at liberty?* She sent back an enthusiastic affirmative and her location, and a short time later was rewarded with a soft knock.

Kerelle practically swept him through the door, her arms locked around his shoulders as it closed behind them with a satisfying *click*. It was only after long moments spent reacquainting herself with the taste of his lips and the softness of his golden hair that she really *looked* at his face.

His eyes were bright as always, but already lines of exhaustion were threaded at their edges. Examining him closer, she could see the weary tilt to his posture, the stress furrowed in his brow. Galhen certainly didn't look like he'd stepped fresh off a transport that morning. Since she knew that he had, in fact, stepped fresh off a transport that morning, his exhaustion pointed to another source.

"You had to push your regenerative powers that far? Already?" It came out a bit more accusatory than she'd intended; she only meant to express her worry. She hadn't expected it to hit him this hard, not this soon.

"You've seen the hospital, Kerelle," he answered softly. "You know how bad it was."

"Yes," she acknowledged, "but I'd thought all that medical equipment you brought with you was meant to do the heavy lifting."

That was, after all, standard procedure for psionic medics. Healing was far more taxing than other psionic abilities, and most regeneratives used their powers to augment and accelerate the effects of conventional equipment.

"It was, but in this case it arrived far too late to help. The field hospital has been critically low on dermal regen gel and bone repair reagent for weeks now, and many injuries were now too far past for them to be effective. There were dozens of soldiers who faced death or disability without psionic healing, and I was the only one who could give it to them."

He crossed the room and lowered himself carefully to her bed, wincing at apparently sore muscles. Seeing her expression, he sighed.

"I'll be all right, darling, truly," he told her gently. "I'll have a migraine tomorrow, but it will pass. It's a small price to pay for saving lives."

"You're right," she conceded as she slipped onto the bed beside him. "And I'm happy you were able to help the wounded. I just worry about you, especially this early in the campaign. There will be a lot of healing to do in the days to come."

"I won't burn myself out," he assured her, eyes holding hers seriously. "This is not my first warzone, and I know how far I can push myself before risking collapse. As you say, there will be a great deal of need, and it will help no one if my powers are unusable for weeks."

"Besides," he added, "we *did* bring a great deal of supplies, and you met Lanri when we landed - she's a C1 regenerative from the Qarinem office assigned as my assistant. Lanri can't do much for catastrophic injuries, of course, but she'll be able to

help speed the effects of the conventional treatments, and we'll be reaching patients early enough for maximum effect. I won't have to lean as heavily on my psionics going forward."

She nodded her understanding, though her concern lingered. Any psionic could overstress their powers and suffer burnout, losing their abilities for weeks or months while they recovered, but regeneratives suffered it more often than most.

Still, he was right - this wasn't his first warzone. She had to trust that he knew what he was doing. It was also somewhat reassuring to know he wasn't the only regenerative on the medical team, even if the other was only a class-1.

She changed gears. "What was your impression of the juniors on the way over here?'

He shrugged. "We didn't exactly have a heart to heart, but they seemed promising. Lanri has prior warzone experience as well, which will help. I don't think your two are quite as seasoned but they certainly don't lack enthusiasm."

"A little *too* much enthusiasm in some ways," she replied with a rueful chuckle. "I was hoping a six-hour shuttle ride with you might have worn off some of the C3 mystery."

He laughed. "Apologies, darling, next time I'll try to be disillusioningly dull." More gently, he added, "If you're really the first C3 telekinetic they've met, you have to expect them to be a bit starstruck."

It was quiet for a moment as she stared up at the ceiling, trying to find the right words.

"Sometimes I envy them," she said finally. "The lower rankings."

He regarded her with some surprise. "You do realize that we are quite the favored children of the PsiCorp. Many C1s would give their right arms to be us."

"That's because they don't know what it *really* means to be us." Kerelle hesitated a moment, unsure if she really wanted to

share this. But it was *Galhen* - if there were anyone she was safe with, it was him.

She pulled up her memory of that awful first assignment on Elekar, the village that she'd destroyed for Helneres to make a point and strike fear. After a moment's hesitation, she shared it through their bond. His arms tightened around her as it played through both their minds, but he said nothing - merely wrapped her in feelings of warmth and home.

"No C1 would ever be asked to do that," she said finally. "No C1 would be able to."

"True," he agreed quietly, and for a moment it was silent still. Finally he propped himself up on an elbow to look at her, his voice still gentle. "But they also wouldn't get assigned to operate independently for months at a time, or be trusted to lead missions and carry out initiatives with no company handlers hovering over their shoulders. With our burdens comes autonomy."

His eyes held hers. "We get the freedom to make decisions, affect outcomes, see the universe. Imagine being a C1 telepath and being leased out as a personal secretary to men like Helneres."

She gave a snort of disgust. "I'd rather *not* imagine it, thank you." Still, she wasn't quite ready to concede the point. "That's easy for you to say, though. The decisions *you* make save people. I kill them."

"You try not to. You could have leveled that village in half the time, without regard to those trapped inside. You tried to get them clear."

"And now they can starve to death instead of being crushed." She sighed. "I'm sorry I'm being so difficult. I haven't seen you in months and here I am trying to start an argument. The stress of this whole wretched campaign is getting to me."

He kissed her lightly. "Darling, you have nothing to apologize for."

He opened himself fully to their bond then, offering her his thoughts and feelings without reservation. How much he cared for her, the joy it brought him to see her face again, the contentment he felt to simply hold her in his arms. She stroked his hair softly and did the same, folding away her mental defenses in a way she could never contemplate with anyone else.

They lay for a moment, simply basking in the feeling of oneness. The dream was a treasured gift, a way to be together when they might otherwise spend months or years apart. But it was still a pale substitute for actually lying in each others' arms. It could imitate touch and speech, but not the heady glow of the fully open bond, not the enfolding warmth of knowing her lover saw each broken piece of herself and treasured them.

She wasn't sure which of them moved first, only that her lips were pressed to his, the buttons of her shirt unfastening as she worked his jacket over his shoulders. Soon enough there were no layers left between them, only lips and hands and soft bare skin to touch.

Kerelle drifted slowly to sleep afterwards, tucked in the spot between his chest and shoulder that seemed perfectly fitted to her form. Here like this, the Elekar war and her duties to SysTech seemed far away, as though she had taken shelter somewhere they could not follow. If she held still and blocked them out, she might almost be herself again - the herself she had been, before SysTech had made her a weapon. The herself that died a bit more with every assignment.

It was a temporary reprieve only. It wouldn't, couldn't last. But right in this moment she felt safe and cherished, and she could pretend the world ended outside this room. So she shut her eyes, and let Galhen's steady heartbeat lull her to sleep.

All too soon, morning came, and it was back to work.

AS IT TURNED OUT, Galhen's group had been the last of the reinforcements to arrive. There was little left to do in Albant but finish consolidating troops and supplies, and two days later the Security Force departed their erstwhile haven.

Or rather, *most* of the Security Force departed. A small garrison was remaining behind in Albant, ostensibly to protect the settlement from the rebels. That was the reason Commander Zereyl had given the council, and that they had smilingly thanked him for.

It wasn't the real reason, naturally. SysTech had gotten what it needed from Albant; it didn't give a rat's ass if they were fire-bombed by vengeful rebels now. The garrison was there to ensure the town and the council didn't have any second thoughts about their allegiance once the main force had moved on. Kerelle wasn't sure if it even counted as an open secret, at this point. Zereyl knew it, and the council knew it, and the citizens hurrying past with averted gazes knew it. There was no one for it to be secret *from*.

Everyone played their part in maintaining the polite fiction anyway. Albant had been committed to this course the moment they'd opened their gates.

Kerelle was going to miss Dalsen's bathtub, but otherwise she left Albant behind with few regrets. Whatever the future had in store for this town, there was nothing she could do to affect it. Her assignment was to help bring the Elekar conflict to a close, and that meant moving forward. The large, rugged eastern provinces would not capitulate as easily as Albant.

But the sooner they did, the sooner she and Galhen got to go home.

———

THEY MADE it four days before the first attack.

The scraggly woods had made her uncomfortable from the

start. There was no going around them, they stretched for too far and the terrain was too rugged for their supply transports to leave the road. All the same, the woods offered too much cover to anyone that might be lurking nearby. She wasn't the only one who thought so - the soldiers who had been on Elekar from the beginning glanced uneasily over their shoulders. They hadn't forgotten those early disasters any more than she had.

When it came, the only warning was a faint twang of ill-intent against her senses. It was enough; after months on Elekar, Kerelle knew not to hesitate.

"Ambush!" She threw the shield up before the word had left her mouth, hoping she had enough coverage to fend off the imminent attack. From the shaky read she'd gotten on their location, the rebels would be on them in seconds.

She sent Galhen the only mental energy she could spare, overlaid with urgency. *Get under cover - we're being attacked.* He was with the medical team, further behind in the column - Kerelle only had time for a fleeting desperate regret that she was not there to protect him directly before the first volley hit.

Deafening cracks filled the air as the small thrown explosives detonated against her shield. Kerelle grimaced and dug her feet in as the impact threatened to send her wobbling. Almost immediately, bullets began to ping off her defenses, flying out from every direction in the woods.

Suddenly the pressure receded as another shield sprung up around hers, absorbing some of the force. Selon had come up beside her while she'd been distracted by holding off the explosives; he gave her a tight nod and strengthened their defenses, face creased in concentration. Spent bullets were beginning to accumulate in the road around them like a terrible snow.

Alna squeezed past a pair of soldiers to sprint into Kerelle's field of view. A small cloud of the rebel's explosive devices followed her, floating high above their shields.

"Caught these in the volley, ma'am." Her eager eyes gleamed. "Back at them?"

Trusting Selon to hold the shields, Kerelle pulled her attention back to the troops around them and looked for Zereyl. He had been nearby before the ambush struck - there. The commander had rallied the troops into a defensive formation while they were busy with the projectiles. He met her eyes immediately with the unspoken question of whether it was safe to fire back.

"Hold position until we signal," Kerelle shouted to him above the din. "We'll maintain shields and flush them out, then be ready to finish things." He nodded his understanding and started issuing the orders. Kerelle turned back to Alna.

"Follow my targets. We'll aim to break their formations and push them out of cover." Alna gave a decisive nod, and Kerelle spread her senses to the angry, determined minds that surrounded them. They were spread out around the column, but there was definitely a higher concentration of people near her. The rebels had probably been hoping to overwhelm and take out the psionics, then harry the rest of the column.

Well, that had been optimistic of them.

Kerelle reached out with her telekinetics to pluck a few of Alna's floating bombs from the younger woman's psionic grasp. Before any of their attackers could realize the plan, she hurled them towards where she'd sensed the biggest group of rebels. Alna's explosives followed only centimeters behind.

The blast of the combined bombs shook the woods around them, its concussive force buffeting Selon's shield with splintered wood. The rebels had no such barrier to protect them, and screams echoed far beyond the initial blast radius. Fear and panic began to spread through the rebels' auras, and they began to scatter.

This was their chance to finish it.

"Commander, they're retreating!" Kerelle shouted to Zereyl. "Pursuit?"

"Yes." He shouted his own orders to the soldiers around him. "Enemy is retreating, prepare to advance and eliminate."

Kerelle turned her attention back to her telekinetics. "Selon, maintain shields around supplies and medical, at the signal drop the barrier around everything else. Alna, we'll advance with the troops. Focus on eliminating hostiles that pose the biggest threat, and cutting off escape where possible." She readied her own telekinetics; a second later Zereyl gave the signal.

It was over quickly. The shredded woods near where the bombs had hit offered little cover to their erstwhile ambushers, and those that kept ahead of the soldiers were brought down by Kerelle and Alna. It seemed the rebels had been relying heavily on using the element of surprise to inflict maximum damage.

A month ago, it might have been enough to leave their column in bloodied disarray, further straining what remained of their medical supplies. This time, their increased firepower and Selon's dedicated shielding meant the casualties were overwhelmingly on the rebel side. The few SysTech wounded were treated by Galhen and Lanri. There had been no deaths.

The winds were changing for the Elekar war.

FIVE

IF SYSTECH HAD SENT adequate resources in the first place, Kerelle mused, the entire Elekar campaign might have been over in half the time.

The two months since they had departed Albant had proved decisive. The main SysTech force had pushed deeply into the rebel-aligned eastern province, and they had already rooted out several hidden outposts. Zereyl suspected the region's largest village was providing material support - which was why their force was now camped beside it. At least Helneres wasn't here to demand a demolition.

She wandered idly through the camp, at rare loose ends. There would be more to do soon, when the scouts returned with more precise intel on the location of the remaining rebel outpost Command suspected was nearby. Until then, she was more or less at liberty. Her feet took her to the field hospital.

The medical tents were arranged in a neat square, creating a small complex within the larger camp. The largest tent held beds for the wounded, with several smaller ones serving as makeshift surgery theaters or administrative offices. None were particularly full - between increased intelligence resources, more comprehensive PsiCorp support and a better-supplied medical team, casualties had sharply dropped.

Kerelle made her way to the small tent that served as Galhen's personal office. It was easy to spot - it was the one with the anxious Elekari clustered outside.

There were nearly a dozen of them, their thin frames and hollow faces a stark reminder that the chaos of the war had pushed many Elekari farmers from subsistence to starvation. An uncomfortable-looking young soldier watched them from the side of the tent as they huddled together with their eyes on the ground. Kerelle could pick up their emotions from across the square - despair from some, hope from others, fear from all.

A young woman emerged from Galhen's office-tent holding a sleeping child, and hurriedly walked past the other assembled Elekari, cheeks hot and eyes averted. Her unexpectedly loud jumble of thoughts nearly slapped Kerelle in the face. She couldn't go home now, her brother will throw her out for this. She went to *them*, went to one of their *witches*, with her husband dead fighting them and her nephews starving because *they* burned the crops. But she had to, she'd do it again, Felhi is going to *live* and that's all that matters and surely Tanlen's ghost isn't angry, he'd want Felhi to live too...

Kerelle strengthened her mental barriers to mute the retreating woman's thoughts, narrowly stopping herself from stepping backwards out of reflex. Galhen's voice echoed through their bond with a shade of reprimand. *And this is why we increase shields around patients, darling.* He'd followed the woman out, flanked by his C1 aide, and was now facing the small group outside with a calm, welcoming smile.

"Thank you for waiting. How many of you were here about a cough?" Most of the Elekari cautiously raised their hands. "Have any of you experienced bloody phlegm when coughing?" This time just two, both looking wan. The others sidled away from them.

"It's all right, it's very treatable, and we'll have you healthy again in no time," he reassured them, projecting openness and warmth. "The two of you can come in with me, and my assistant Lanri will be able to help the rest of you." The young C1 stepped up to the group to introduce herself as Galhen ushered the two bloody-cough Elekari into his office. *You can come in if you like, this won't take long.*

Kerelle took the invitation and followed them into the office, awkwardly perching on a seat in a corner. Galhen was friendly but efficient, giving each patient a quick examination that seemed to confirm whatever he thought it was. With each, he ended up lightly resting his fingers just below their collarbone, his eyes unfocusing for several long minutes. When he removed his hand, his patient was breathing audibly easier.

When the Elekari had departed, clutching the ration bars he'd pressed into their hands on the way out, Galhen sank down into his desk chair and glanced over at her. *I hope that's the last of that for awhile, but I'm afraid it won't be. Particularly if Helneres keeps rebuffing my recommendations for importing food.*

Did they all have the same thing?

Yes. Phyletria. It's not usually serious in healthy adults, but for cold, starving people with weak immune systems it can be deadly. After I saw two cases in a row, I thought we might as well expedite things. Fortunately for most of them it wasn't advanced - Lanri will be able to take care of it for them without difficulty.

Those people you treated though, the ones who were coughing blood...would they have died?

Yes.

Galhen sighed deeply and produced a small bottle of dark amber something from his desk. "They might still," he admitted as he poured a glass. "I eliminated the virus and did what I could to boost their immune systems, but they're both weak from it still, and who knows what else is floating around the village." He grimaced. "As you saw, many are reluctant to have anything to do with us, even for free health care. And I can't blame them." Galhen took a long sip and offered her the bottle. "Whiskey?"

She took it, and the glass that followed. She closed her eyes at the smooth burn; it was top shelf, and by far the best thing she'd drunk in nearly a year. *You brought this with you? You've been holding out on me.*

Emergencies only, darling. I couldn't fit that much of it in my pack.

The smile didn't reach his eyes, and when he spoke again his voice was laced with frustration.

"I've written Helneres several times about this, but he won't see reason. It's all self-righteous proclamations that they should have thought of this before rebelling, and he's not going to waste funds 'insulating them from consequences.' If he could see more than ten minutes into the future, he might see that it will cost more later if all his miners are coughing up their lungs this winter, or if he ends up having to import *everything* because the civilian population collapses."

"I'm surprised he's letting you treat the Elekari at all."

"Oh, he has no idea, somehow I keep forgetting to mention it. He'd be furious if he did, but fortunately none of us *actually* report to him, do we?" He clinked her glass. "Worst he can do is file a complaint with Director Cafora, who will agree with me on the long-term company benefit of preventing further workforce destabilization."

"You've put some thought into this."

His smile was bitter. "Well, 'saving human lives' never gets much traction with management. I've learned to get creative."

He knocked back his glass. "Honestly though? The best thing we could do for the health and safety of the Elekari is get our forces off the planet. Things won't get better for them until we do."

THE INTELLIGENCE OFFICER flicked the projection screen to an overview map of the province, a red circle indicating a point of interest.

"We've scouted exhaustively and found no other evidence of enemy camps. Our last sweep appears to have been effective in eliminating any outlying pockets." He pointed again at the circled location, nestled in the mountains on the projected map. "We believe that virtually all their remaining forces are concentrated here."

"Captain, the theme of this campaign has been rebel misdirection and concealment. Every time we think we have them, out pop more from yet another hidey-hole. What makes this time any different?" The vidscreen lent Helneres's voice a slightly tinny quality, but still managed to capture his trademark oily condescension. Naturally he was attending the meeting remotely, from the comfort of his mansion in the capital.

"In the months since reinforcements arrived, sir, our forces have kept considerable pressure on the rebels. We've captured several of their operation centers, and as you know we were able to identify and subsequently eliminate influential members of their leadership, particularly Rhalen Karek Ausa."

"Yes, captain, I *do* know that, you may recall I had the old headman shot when we learned he'd concealed his son's involvement. Are you just going to regurgitate events back to me or do you have a point?"

The intelligence officer's face and tone stayed consummately professional, without a hint of the irritation Kerelle sensed welling up behind his calm facade. "My point, sir, is that we have crippled both their operations and their recruiting ability. The PsiCorp," he nodded at Kerelle, "have done excellent work discouraging opposition, and with Ausa dead they don't have a charismatic leader to whip up the populace against us. All evidence indicates their numbers are substantially reduced from the start of the summer and are not replenishing.

"Additionally," he continued, moving his pointer to indicate surrounding areas, "we have curtailed multiple efforts by rebel forces to move supplies in the vicinity of their stronghold. We've also arrested any forays out of the immediate areas, and they seem to have refocused on fortifications. In short, we have them pinned down, unable to resupply, and there is every indication they are preparing for a last stand."

"Then why haven't we crushed them yet?" Helneres managed to sound both bored and accusing. Expressions around the room did not change, but their projected thoughts made it clear Kerelle wasn't the only one who silently wished he would just hang up already so they could actually make some progress on all this. Galhen's telepathic eyeroll was particularly pronounced, overlaid with shades of his general contempt for the governor.

Once again the intelligence officer did not react; Kerelle wondered how much of his career had been spent dealing with self-important executives.

"As stated, sir, we have successfully executed on our strategic initiative to eliminate any remaining resistance in the surrounding region, thus concentrating the surviving forces inside their stronghold. With that now complete, we are ready for a final strike." He immediately flicked the projection to a more detailed image of the area, annotated with proposed troop movements. Kerelle suspected it was to move on before Helneres had a chance to interrupt again.

"We expect it will not be an easy assault. The fortress is well-positioned in the mountains, with the only access through narrow passes.The rebels have made heavy use of traps throughout the campaign and they've had time to prepare for us. We expect significant casualties. However, this is our best chance to end the insurgency and ensure stability on Elekar, once and for all."

"ER, MA'AM?"

Kerelle concealed her start of surprise at Alna's sudden appearance at her shoulder. It was late, she had expected both the juniors would have retired for the night - or at least be occupied with something more interesting than talking to her. She'd met with them both shortly after the strategy session adjourned to explain the upcoming assault, and the part their group would play in it. They knew the coming attack was going to be hard.

All the more reason it was odd Alna was here instead of taking advantage of the last relatively comfortable night in the main camp. Frankly Kerelle was hoping to retire for the night herself, preferably nestled against Galhen, but duty called. She set her face in a professional smile and turned to meet the junior agent.

"Yes, Alna? Is there something I can help with?"

"Yes...er...maybe. I hope so, but I understand you're quite busy..." A slight flush rose on the younger woman's cheeks, her eyes on the ground. Kerelle kept her smile in place, though her curiousity was spiking at what had Alna in such an uncharacteristic state. *Stars above, I hope she isn't going to ask me for romantic advice.*

Kerelle had little enough to offer on *that* front; somehow she suspected "be pleasantly surprised and also slightly incredulous when the handsome boy you have a crush on also has a crush on you" wasn't advice anyone would find helpful.

But as it turned out, it wasn't relationship concerns that had Alna fidgeting uncomfortably. It was something far more delicate.

"Ma'am, I..." Alna took a deep breath. "I want to start with how much of an honor this has been, to be able to serve under you and learn from you. I feel like I know so much more now than when I got here, not just how to fight but how to work with the Security Force, and I..." her flush deepened. "Thank you. Ma'am."

"You're very welcome, Alna." Kerelle waited. She doubted that was why the younger telekinetic had sought her out.

"It's just I...I'm giving it my all, *of course*," Alna hurried through the words, as if desperate to head off any thoughts that she was holding back in her efforts. "But I....haven't had many assignments like this one, and it's been...it's been harder than I thought it would be. Just...with everything." She was rushing now, as if she were afraid that stopping for breath would mean losing her nerve. "And I don't ever want to let feelings affect my work, and I'm trying to do what they taught us in the Academy but it's not the same as it was in school and I was..." she swallowed. "I was wondering if you had any advice for me. About that. Ma'am."

Kerelle paused.

"MA'AM?"

The older woman smiled at her. "Yes, Kerelle?"

She hesitated, suddenly unsure. Maybe it was inappropriate to bring this up at all. But Ms. Belnesar was her favorite of her teachers, and she'd always seeemed fond of Kerelle. Surely if she could talk about this with anyone, she could talk about it with her.

"I'm...I'm worried about what's going to happen soon. When I leave the Academy."

"Worried?" Ms. Belnesar cocked her head. "Kerelle, you're a very talented girl, and you're one of my top students. You have nothing to worry about. You'll excel at any assignment you're given."

"It's not that," Kerelle conceded reluctantly. "It's more...about the work itself. About fighting with the Security Force. I'm...I'm not sure I'm going to do well." Realizing how it sounded, she rushed on. "I mean I want to do well, of course! And I know it's my duty, and I don't want to

disappoint the company after everything they've done for me! It's just...
actually using my powers against...against people*..."*

Ms. *Belnesar nodded, face full of sympathy.* "I know, Kerelle. *It's*
hard, sometimes, and you have one of the more challenging roles in the
PsiCorp. But you wouldn't have made it this far if we didn't all believe in
you."

"But what if I let everyone down?" What if I can't do it, when the
time comes?

"You won't," she answered reassuringly. *"I know you, Kerelle. You'll*
do the right thing when you need to."

"It doesn't always feel like the right thing," she whispered. *This was*
dangerous ground, now, more dangerous than a crisis of confidence.

Ms. *Belnesar sighed and drew Kerelle into a loose hug, resting her chin*
on her shoulder. "It doesn't, and that's part of what makes your role so
hard. Following your duty takes a lot of discipline sometimes, especially
when you have emotions telling you something else. But remember that if
the company asks you to do something, it's because there's a reason, *even*
if we can't see it ourselves."

She pulled back to look Kerelle in the eyes, a gentle smile on her lips.
"Sometimes things seem *wrong, because we only see a small part of the*
picture. But remember that the people higher up from us can see the big
picture. When you get your orders to do something, it's because a lot of
very smart people, who can see the big picture, determined that that thing
needed to happen in order for the big picture to turn out right."

Ms. *Belnesar squeezed Kerelle's hands.* "I know it's tempting some-
times to just hide away from duty, especially when it means we have to
make sacrifices. But you're stronger than that, Kerelle. I know you won't
let fear and doubt control you. When the time comes," she added encour-
agingly, "I know you'll do the right thing, always."

KERELLE KNEW the correct things to say to Alna; it was what
Ms. Belnesar had told her a dozen-odd years prior, about duty

and understanding and discipline. It wouldn't even be the first time she'd repeated them. But as she stared back at the younger woman and saw her teenage self reflected in Alna's worried eyes, the words died on her lips.

She couldn't stand here on the eve of the battle for Elekar and tell her everything was all right, that they were here for any bigger reason than SysTech's bottomless greed. They weren't.

"It doesn't get easier," Kerelle answered honestly instead. "You just get numb."

Alna took a step back, clearly nonplussed. She'd probably been expecting the hug and the reassurance that there was a reason behind it all. But those things weren't going to help her, any more than they'd ever helped Kerelle. And while Alna might be only a C2, she was very talented. Her career was going to look a lot like Kerelle's did.

"I'm not going to bullshit you," Kerelle told her bluntly. "We have the hardest job in the PsiCorp, and it's because of assignments like this. Elekar won't be the last, for either of us. And it's all right that you don't feel good about it. In fact, you *shouldn't* feel good about it, because there is nothing good about what's happening here."

She shouldn't be saying all this, not out loud, not to someone she'd only known a few months. But they were alone here in the stifling dark of the Elekar night, with only the faint stars above as witness, and she didn't have it in her to lie.

"How do *you* do it then?" Alna's question was almost a whisper.

My lover kisses away my tears and tells me I'm not a monster, and I no longer entirely believe him. But that wasn't an answer she was willing to share, nor was it likely to be particularly helpful to Alna. Alna, who was trapped in this life just like she was. Kerelle sighed, and tried to think of the right words.

"I have reasons I want to survive," she answered finally, "And I remember that if I ever want to see them again, then this is the only path forward." She was glad Alna wasn't a telepath, as Galhen's face flashed through her mind. "Using our powers against others...it never gets easy, no matter why the mission briefing says it's necessary. But there's nothing we can do to change the company, or the PsiCorp, or the world we live in. All we can do is survive in it."

If Alna had her own forbidden thoughts, she kept them to herself. Wise girl.

"I see," she said finally, her face troubled. Still, her gaze was sincere as she met Kerelle's eyes. "Thank you, ma'am. For telling me." *For not repeating the easy lie,* though she didn't say it aloud.

Kerelle inclined her head slightly. "Get some sleep, Alna. We'll need it in the next few days."

SIX

THE MORNING of the assault dawned cold and clouded. There had been debate about whether to attempt it at night, but with the conditions they were likely to face the increased danger to their troops would outweigh any brief element of surprise they might gain.

Their forces gathered into formation. They would approach in two columns, up the narrow paths that lined either side of the canyon's walls. Selon and Alna took their places at the head of one column. Whatever doubts Alna had had a few nights prior, there were no sign of them now; she and Selon stood silent and resolute, with none of the nervous energy that had marked their first days on Elekar.

Kerelle watched them with a bittersweet sort of pride. They had both firmed up, after four months in the field. She trusted them now, to fulfill their part in this. She was sorry they had to.

As she took her own place, she felt Galhen's soft touch on her mind through their bond. *This is it, then?*

Yes. They're making the final preparations now. Then, because she sensed his worry, *This is what I do, darling.*

I know. And I know you're good at it. I just don't usually get a front row seat. He sent her a burst of warmth and affection and need. *Do what you must, darling. Stay safe and come back to me.*

Kerelle sent him the feeling back and savored the moment of shared warmth. *I will.* She closed her eyes for a moment, then muted their bond.

It was time.

The rebels' fortress appeared to have been built into the rock itself. Kerelle could only assume it predated the rebellion, perhaps a relic of the early days of colonization. Sheer cliffs made up the sides, with only a pair of narrow switchbacked paths leading up to small entrance. She could see why they had chosen here to make their stand.

Kerelle stood near the head of one column, Alna at the other. Selon was beside her on the opposite column from Kerelle; he had shields up before both columns. They waited, poised in the still air of the early dawn.

Commander Zereyl gave the signal.

Kerelle ripped a chunk of rock from the cliffs above and hurled it to the path below. She began rolling it upward, but had hardly gotten more than a short ways before it exploded against the mines sunk in shallow grooves along the path. There was an echoing boom from the other side as Alna did the same. Dust and pebbles rained down from the cliffs, along with chunks of the shattered rock. It bounced harmlessly off the shield and into the canyon below.

Well, they know we're here.

The advance up the paths was deliberate and painfully slow, Kerelle and Alna doing their best to trigger traps before their troops reached them. Selon kept up his shields, and as they drew closer the soft pop of deflected sniper fire joined the cacophony, punctuated by the occasional scream as a shot slipped past. Their own troops could only stay close and make their way up the mountain - the shield would have to come down before they could fire back.

The sun had cleared the top of the cliffs, and the entrance was in sight, when a dark object flying towards them caught Kerelle's eye. She threw up a reinforcing shield in anticipation, but the object simply sailed over their heads - and their shields. It hit the cliff face with a hard *clink*, followed by a deafening boom.

The path shook violently under her feet as a crack sounded overhead, with a thick, ominous roar of shifting earth. Her gut twisted with realization - that explosive hadn't been aimed for *them* at all.

"The cliff! They're collapsing the cliff!" But there was nowhere to go as the rock tumbled forward, an inexorable wave of dirt following. Kerelle had a half-second's thought of trying to hold it back but no, there was too much, the force of it would snap her in half. She ducked into a ball and threw up the strongest shield she could, in as wide as space as she dared, low enough to the ground that the landslide could roll above it. The lucky handful of soldiers that had been in range huddled down with her. She got the barest glimpse of their frightened faces before the ground roared overhead and plunged them all into darkness.

Even with the full force of the landslide passing above them rather than against them, keeping the shield in place was difficult, and sweat ran freely down her face with the effort. Kerelle tried to ignore it and just focus on the task at hand. *Don't think about how hard it is to hold this, don't think about how a crack in the shield will kill us all in minutes,* definitely *don't think about how deep we might already be buried...*

With an effort she shut down her train of thought, narrowing her focus to the shield and her breathing. Breathe in, breathe out, breathe in.

Finally the noise quieted, and her carefully measured breaths suddenly sounded harsh and deafening in the total black. Hers, and those of the soldiers around her - some with the fast cadence of near-panic.

It occurred to her that there probably wasn't a lot of air down here, and she heard her own breathing speed up. She forced it to slow back down. Panic wouldn't help them. She could feel later; she had to get them out first.

"I think the landslide is past," she said quietly. In the small, darkened space, her voice still sounded like a shout. "I'm going to try to dig us out. Be ready to move." A chorus of whispered "yes ma'ams" answered her, along with a flood of projected feelings she had to block out. These people were terrified of dying down here, and desperately trusting her to save them.

Well, she was pretty terrified of dying down here too. Hopefully that trust wasn't misplaced.

She couldn't see anything, but Kerelle closed her eyes anyway in a habit of concentration, and turned all her attention to the earth above them. Burning stars, it was heavy - but she already knew that, it was pressing down on her shields. *Focus, Kerelle.*

All right: if she started to bend the shield upward, there was the risk it would just snap and bury them all anyway. Better to dig down from above and try to clear a small enough section for them to climb out. It would be easier if she could see what she was digging at, but nothing for it. She lifted her hand to touch the top of the shield, and sent a thread of her telekinetics straight up. Ever so carefully, hoping against hope that the additional disturbance wouldn't trigger another landslide, she started to widen the thread.

Time slowed as she painstakingly worked the dirt apart, creating a small open zone held clear by her power. It felt like years that they were down there, and a disconnected part of her mind wondered if it was happening at all - maybe she *had* been buried in the landslide, and all this was just a dying hallucination as her oxygen-starved brain shut down.

But no - suddenly a thin beam of light hit her eyes, almost painful after the oppressive darkness. Her heart sped up. She'd broken through.

"Hang on, everyone," she told the others. "We have to be careful still. But," and even to her own ears, the relief flooding her voice was unmistakable, "we're going to get out."

Pulling herself out of the hole into daylight was almost euphoric. When the last solider wriggled out behind her, Kerelle collapsed the shields down below with a gasp of relief. The weight of them all had been wearing on her, a strain she had become so accustomed to that she felt it more acutely now that it was gone. What she really wanted was to collapse into Dalsen's tub with a cup of tea.

But the day's tasks had hardly begun, and so she settled for leaning against the more stable cliff face as she caught her breath, a few hurried gulps from her canteen helping to wash away the taste of buried dust. Glancing behind them, the path they had taken was now completely impassable, blocked by the fallen cliff. From the looks of things, Selon had deflected the bomb on the other side, and the left path was now the primary route in to the fortress. Judging from the troops she could see, the remnants of the right column and turned around and joined the left side after the path collapsed.

The fortress itself was a swarm of SysTech troops now, sounds of battle carrying out to where they stood resting. There was no going back the path she'd taken up here, but the path forward to the fortress was clear. Clear, and short - they'd been almost at the top when the landslide had hit.

Kerelle took a few steadying breaths and final gulp of water before she pushed herself off the cliff. There was still a job to do, and she was tired but not incapable. She glanced back at her small group of soldiers and got a series of shaky nods. They were thinking the same thing she was.

"Right then," she nodded back. They were all professionals

here. "I'll throw up a shield to block any incoming fire. On my signal, we run up the rest of the path and rejoin the main force."

They did, flowing back into the SysTech attack group at the fortress's blown-off doors. The assault had begun in earnest.

THE NEXT FEW hours were nothing less than a nightmare.

The Elekari rebels knew this was the end, and they fought now to make the SysTech victory as costly as possible. Booby traps and hidden ambushes riddled the maze of narrow tunnels that made up the fortress's interior, and misplaced steps took a high toll on the attacking force. More than one of the rebels simply flung themselves into a knot of SysTech troops, clutching active grenades.

At first Kerelle tried to keep her senses open to detect ambushes, but the close-packed chaos made it nearly impossible - not to mention that inattention to her surroundings could prove deadly. She soon gave up and focused on alternately shielding and attacking, though both were hampered by the narrow twisting corridors. The close quarters created a constant danger of friendly fire, and she worried too hard a blow might bring the whole place down on their heads.

In the end, for all the rebels' grim cleverness and desperate sacrifice, the SysTech numbers were simply too high. As the clouded sky began to tinge orange, the last shots faded and there were only the groans of the wounded and dying among the SysTech force. The rebels had died fighting to a man.

The final group of rebels had made their stand in front of a heavily barricaded door. When the bodies were moved aside and the barricades brought down, the doors were smashed open to reveal a small group of people huddled inside what looked like a command center.

Even through her shielded senses, Kerelle could sense their

terror. She recognized a few of the faces from intelligence briefings; this was the Elekari government-in-exile, and they knew what was going to happen as much as she did. She started walking as the soldiers began lining them against the wall.

She almost made it out of earshot before the guns started up.

Kerelle's feet propelled her forward through halls littered with grey-clad bodies and down steps slick with blood, seized with an overriding need to get out of this oppressive space and into the clean air. She kept her eyes and mind focused on where to put her feet, because otherwise she might look around and *see* what had happened, to people she had marched and camped and eaten with. She dimly registered the sound of her own footsteps picking up speed until finally she cleared the broken doors, and stepped into the fading day.

Outside was improved only by the open canopy of the sky. Here too there had been terrible losses, but at least there was no feeling of being trapped in a mountain of rock and bone.

Selon and Alna had retreated outside as well, and she found them huddled against a rocky outcropping as soldiers bustled around them collecting the fallen. They stared up at her in shaking, hollow-eyed silence, and she was almost bodily struck by how young they were. They'd been confident and eager when they arrived, but Kerelle knew from their records that neither of them had ever seen anything like this.

She knew she should stop and try to comfort them, but she simply could not. She had no comfort to provide, no well of serenity to draw from. The best she could manage was a weary nod of acknowledgement before starting back down the mountain towards camp.

Her tent was a meager sanctuary, but it was all she had. In the fragile privacy of the canvas walls, Kerelle finally let herself collapse into a shaking ball. She wanted desperately to reach for Galhen, but the infirmary must be packed to bursting, and he could not afford to be distracted. Duty first.

She was not asleep when, late in the night, Galhen quietly entered the tent and lay down beside her. She pressed against him as he wrapped trembling arms around her, and they held each other in silence. Even mentally, words were inadequate; instead they let memory and emotion flow through the bond to speak for them. Kerelle didn't have to tell Galhen what the assault was like - he'd seen it in the hospital. From the way his weary hands shook in hers, he'd given much of himself trying to help in the aftermath.

She didn't know how long they lay there, silently pouring out their grief and guilt and horror. The brutal room-to-room fighting, the enemy defiant to the gruesome end. The broken, bloodied soldiers he was able to save, and so many more that he wasn't. Her last thought as she finally drifted off to restless sleep in his arms was simply gratitude that he was with her, solid and loving and real. That this was one nightmare she didn't have to face alone.

SEVEN

THE AUTUMN WINDS were growing teeth, Kerelle thought as she shivered in a particularly sharp gust. Elekar's sparse foliage had long since lost whatever color it had managed during the summer, and the always-stark landscape began to take on the look of a dead world.

The comparison felt uncomfortably apt. The final tally of the war's casualties estimated that there were now more people buried in Elekar's mass graves than walking its surface. The true number might never be known. Across the planet, grey dust settled on recently-turned soil, enclosing rebel and SysTech alike. Were they marked, one could have shadowed the campaign's progress by following their placement, but they were not marked. Nobody wanted to remember.

She checked her pack one last time, with a moment's sober meditation on how lucky she was. In an hour's time a transport would touch down and carry her away from Elekar, most likely forever, and back to Tallimau and all its comforts. In a few weeks she would be ensconced back in the city, sipping wine and deciding which delicacy to order for dinner. The Elekari whose world this was, except for the parts that were valuable, would be staring down winter amidst shattered infrastructure and empty food stores. She ought to feel some sort of triumph for ending the war, or at least relief at leaving. Instead she only felt hollow.

Galhen met her at the dock, his own pack neatly arranged and at the ready. She greeted him with a smile. There was that to look forward to - since they were both returning to Tallimau, they would take the transport together. And after that, a few glorious weeks of coinciding leave. Kerelle should be happy about that, and she knew she would be once they got underway, but it was hard to stand here in the Elekari dust and feel anything but emptiness.

She knew Galhen understood. A pulse of regret through their bond told her he felt the same.

"Agent Evandra!" Kerelle turned to see Alna approaching at a energetic clip, Selon at her heels. She pulled up short in front of Kerelle and saluted, and for a moment she looked like the eager novice she'd been six months earlier. But there were shadows under her eyes that hadn't been there before, and Kerelle could sense that unease hung on both the junior agents like a shroud. They would try to bury it when they left, under luxury and pleasure and the cover of duty, but Elekar would scar them too.

"Agent Evandra, Agent Ambrel." Alna inclined her head slightly to Galhen before returning her attention to Kerelle. "Our transport to Uliste is almost here. We wanted to say goodbye before we left."

Kerelle made herself smile, willing her dark thoughts away from her expression. "It was a pleasure to work with both of you," she said sincerely. "Alna, Selon, you both did very well. I'll be writing the Uliste director to tell him how pleased I was with your performance."

Alna's smile reached her eyes for the first time. "Thank you ma'am. For... for everything."

The transport's chimes rang out for passengers-aboard. The two juniors gave her hasty nods and waved as they sped back to their ride home. Kerelle watched them go, and hoped for their own sake that their memories of what happened here were as easy to leave behind.

It was not long after that the transport to Tallimau arrived, and they loaded in. Ten months and twelve days after she arrived, Kerelle watched Elekar's grey surface retreat beneath them, and finally vanish altogether under the haze of clouds.

AS THE TRANSPORT dipped down through the clear skies, Tallimau's glittering skyscrapers rose up to welcome them back. Towering structures covered most of the planet's surface, with only the inky oceans and patches of green parkland breaking up the endless city blocks. Perhaps once in the distant past they had been separate townships with separate names, but all had long since run together into the megalopolis that now shared its name with the planet itself.

As always, Kerelle had mixed feelings at the sight of it. Tallimau was the closest she had to a home, sort of. It was the location of her manager and her residence suite, at least - though her frequent field work meant she saw little of either.

For Galhen, who had lived on the Tallimau PsiCorp base since childhood, it *was* home - and sure enough, his burst of affection for the sight of that shining landscape echoed through the bond as they descended. Kerelle never entirely understood it, but then, she'd never seen his original home of Istel City. Maybe he'd always lived in landscapes like this.

Tallimau no longer overwhelmed her, as it had the first time she'd seen it as a teenager. Kerelle had been transferred there for advanced training after spending her childhood at the more rural Hasha base. Her first time touching down in the dense forest of skyscrapers, with only stolen snatches of sky visible between their edges, had felt like being trapped in a shining metal box.

She was used to it now, of course. But even after fifteen years of being stationed here, she'd still never quite warmed to the megalopolis, at once packed with humanity and cold with steel and glass. It wasn't that she didn't like cities - she did, quite a bit. She just preferred them to feel slightly less enclosed.

Well, they didn't have to stay here the whole time. After almost a year in a war zone - plus Galhen's previous stint at a medical disaster site - they each had enough leave for a trip to an offworld resort. Kerelle could smell the beach breeze already.

It was duty first, of course, when they returned to base. Check-ins were made, reports were filed, debrief meetings were attended. There was that letter of commendation to write to the Uliste director, praising his agents' performance in a very challenging environment. But finally, their time was their own. Kerelle intended to savor it.

THE METRO DOORS swished shut behind them, depositing them in one of the more fashionable of the city's districts. Soft lights twinkled from trees and shop windows as crowds swirled and eddied past, lending the busy streets a welcoming glow. Despite the crowds, Kerelle and Galhen had no difficulty making their way down the avenue. The presence of the PsiCorp base on Tallimau meant its citizens were relatively accustomed to the sight of psionics, but they still didn't necessarily want to get close. Still, there were fewer stares than they would get most anywhere else.

They were seated at an artisanal coffee shop with a breathtaking view of the city, and their order was taken by a young woman whose eyes only once flicked nervously to their collars. As they settled in, Kerelle could sense an excited energy shimmering through their bond. She smiled and lifted an eyebrow.

"Well, are you going to tell me?"

Galhen grinned back at her and slid his tablet across the table. He'd pulled up a news article: *Olstenfel University Appoints New Head of Biotech Division*. Kerelle scanned the text and quickly found what had sparked his interest.

At 37, Dr. Nalea Tarau Ambrel is the youngest to ever fill the prestigious chair…

There was a small photo of Dr. Nalea Tarau Ambrel included with the article. Even at the low resolution, her resemblance to Galhen was unmistakable.

"This is your sister, isn't it?"

His smile practically glowed. "It is. Even when we were little she loved books and school. I shouldn't be surprised she made a career out of it."

His face turned a bit wistful then, and he switched to telepathy. *And it's just nice to know that… that they were all right, you know? I assumed they must have been, my parents didn't fight at all, SysTech had no reason to harm them. Still, it's good to* know.

Because of course he wouldn't have known otherwise; one of the PsiCorp's strictest rules was no contact with the family you'd been taken from.

Still, as Kerelle sent back feelings of agreement, she couldn't quite relate. Galhen had been eight when corporate examiners came to his school to administer a strange test. A few days later several serious men in impeccable suits had arrived at his house; after a short closed-door conversation with his parents they'd left with Galhen. It was a fairly typical PsiCorp story, except for his age. The normal range for psionic powers to manifest was between ages four and nine, so Galhen had been a relative late bloomer - and thus had had more of a childhood than most of their peers.

Kerelle, for her part, only remembered the PsiCorp, with nothing but vague and fleeting impressions of what her life must have been before then. She didn't even have the customary patronymic - whoever from SysTech had taken her either didn't know who her father was, or hadn't bothered to record it. Intellectually she understood it might be easier, not to *know* what she was missing, but it didn't stop a familiar tug of jealousy.

The coffee came out then, and Kerelle took a moment just to breathe it in. She'd nearly forgotten what good coffee was like. She glanced up to see Galhen was watching her closely. He raised his own cup in a toast, eyes holding hers.

"To making it back," he said softly, a bittersweet twinge through their bond.

"To making it back," she echoed quietly. He reached across the table to take her hand in his, when they were interrupted by the sharp beep of his comm.

They both frowned at it - they ought to have several weeks' leave before coming up for reassignment. Still frowning, Galhen reached for the comm.

"Ambrel here," he answered tersely. Kerelle gently stroked the hand that still held hers.

"Ambrel, it's Cafora." Kerelle's frown deepened. Director Cafora oversaw all of the SysTech PsiCorp stationed on the planet. He'd already gotten hers and Galhen's reports, what else could he want so soon?

"I need you back at headquarters for a meeting within the hour. Look presentable." Galhen lifted his eyebrows at Kerelle, keeping his voice carefully neutral as he responded.

"Understood sir. I'm assuming this is about the assignment on Elekar - should Agent Evandra report as well?"

"It's not about Elekar, Ambrel. Agent Evandra isn't involved. Be in my office by sixteen-hundred." The comm clicked as Director Cafora disconnected, leaving Galhen and Kerelle staring at it.

He finally broke the silence. "I guess we won't be savoring this coffee."

KERELLE SHIFTED RESTLESSLY, unable to focus on the article she'd been trying to read for the last half-hour. Whatever Cafora had called Galhen in for, it hadn't sounded good. He'd muted the bond before reporting in, so she had only her own worries to speculate on.

Those worries were intensifying as time crawled forward. It was within Cafora's authority to activate their collars, whether for discipline or termination. But surely that was ridiculous. She did not have a close relationship with Cafora - she tried to avoid his direct attention as much as possible - but in her fifteen years at Tallimau, she'd never known him to be harsh or unfair. Businesslike and no-nonsense, certainly, but not the type to turn first to the torture of the collars for a discipline issue. Besides, Galhen had had more interaction with him, and Kerelle thought they had something of a rapport. Surely that would count for something?

That was even assuming this was about discipline at all. But what could it be? Even if Helneres *had* filed a complaint about how Galhen ran the hospital, and if Galhen had been wrong about Cafora siding with him, she would expect that to be a verbal reprimand.

She was being silly; there was no reason to believe there was any danger at all. Cafora's clipped tone could simply have been a reflection of how busy he was. Besides, Galhen was a rare double-C3, dedicated to his work and, most importantly, intelligent enough to be reliably submissive to PsiCorp managers. He was a model agent in every way. Except one.

This couldn't be about her, could it? Their relationship might be discreet, but it was hardly a *secret* - secrets were an invitation for trouble. Attachments like theirs might be frowned on, but they weren't forbidden, and Kerelle and Galhen both had been very careful not to let their personal involvement influence their work. Besides, if Cafora was taking issue with their romantic status, wouldn't Kerelle be disciplined as well?

Kerelle?

She started, nearly falling off the bed. Relief flooded her at the sound of Galhen's voice, though their bond stayed oddly mute.

You're all right? What was that all about?

He was silent for a moment.

Can you....can you come to my quarters?

She sent her affirmative, her unease trickling back. She nearly ran the few halls to his door.

Tension clenched her at Galhen's ashen face, and his continued psychic silence. He drew her over to the bed, taking a seat on the edge.

She met his vivid green eyes, waiting. He exhaled deeply and leaned forward.

"Kerelle, I..." he trailed off, and his gaze dropped. He stared at the bed for a moment, then closed his eyes and opened the bond.

The shock was almost physical, as if someone had struck her hard in the guts. Numb, staring shock, and under it a hollow despair. She met his eyes again in confused horror, and he leaned forward to rest his brow against hers. She let him pull her into his memory.

Galhen held himself at attention, eyes straight ahead as Director Cafora exchanged pleasantries with their guest and poured her a cup of tea. The middle-aged woman was the representative of a Senator Dalanva in the Morafer system; what she was here for or what any of this had to do with Galhen, Cafora had not deigned to share. He assumed Senator Dalanva was a prospective SysTech client.

"Thank you, Director," their guest was saying. She was dressed professionally, but from what he could see of the cut and quality Galhen estimated she was wearing well over a thousand credits. If her subordinates could afford Pirina handbags, Dalanva's financial wherewithal was clearly significant. No wonder Cafora had wanted this meeting without delay.

The woman sipped her tea and continued. "Is this the man in question?"

Cafora made an affirmative gesture, waving at Galhen. "Ms. Pomia, this is Agent Galhen Tarau Ambrel. Class 3 telepath, Class 3 regenerative, ten years' experience in field operations." Galhen inclined his head in greeting, maintaining his stance. SysTech had two guidelines for PsiCorp meeting clients - military posture unless explicitly told otherwise, and silence unless explicitly questioned.

Ms. Pomia smiled back at him. "And just as pretty as his file photo. Those eyes! Senator Dalanva will be pleased." Galhen kept his gaze straight ahead, careful to conceal his twinge of unease. This wasn't sounding like a typical assignment.

"Glad to hear it, Ms. Pomia. I take it the purchase is confirmed?"

"Certainly, Director. Given his designation and service record, I think we can waive any test of abilities. Class 3 certainly speaks for itself, doesn't it?"

"Indeed - and I imagine his capabilities will be more than sufficient for anything that may arise. Unless, of course, these legislative meetings are more eventful than I've been led to believe." Ms. Pomia laughed politely as Galhen's alarm grew. This was not a typical assignment. Finally, Cafora addressed him directly.

"Ambrel, as Ms. Pomia has confirmed, Senator Dalanva is purchasing a permanent lease on your contract with SysTech. You will serve on her personal staff as a communications specialist, and in whatever other capacity she sees fit. Do whatever you need to prepare tonight. You depart with Ms. Pomia tomorrow morning."

The scene in her mind shifted; when it cleared again the meeting had ended, and Galhen was a few paces behind Cafora in one of the base's corridors.

There had to be some kind of mistake.

Galhen had expected Cafora to follow up with him with some sort of explanation, but instead the Director just walked out checking his messages as if that had been a meeting like any other, as if the entire world *hadn't just shattered. A moment's hesitation, then Galhen hastened his own steps to catch up.*

"Sir?"

"Mm?" Cafora's distant response indicated surprise at the interruption. That was not promising but Galhen couldn't simply leave it, not with the magnitude of what had happened. He'd always had a positive relationship with the Director, surely they could talk about this?

"Sir, I'm not sure I entirely understand."

Eyebrows up then, with a touch of you're-wasting-my-time. "What part was unclear, Ambrel? Senator Dalanva bought a lease on your contract, you'll leave with her aide tomorrow. I would have thought you would want to be making your goodbyes right now."

"Sir, I just thought…My understanding was that Class 3 is not usually leased to civilians. This is… unexpected, especially considering my value to our operations. "

Cafora's eyebrows went higher, and this time his tone held a note of warning. "This was a decision by senior management as the best direction for the business. The Senator made an offer specifically to lease a C3, and it was the highest in company history. We provided a list of C3 agents, she selected you. There isn't anything to discuss."

He turned back to his messages and continued unhurried down the corridor, leaving Galhen to stare after him.

The vision faded, and she could only stare uncomprehending. Permanent lease. Oh, theoretically it had always been a possibility. Sometimes rather than commanding its psionics directly, SysTech leased their contracts to third parties for a large sum. It was common enough for the lower rankings - anyone of any status leased out a C1 telepath secretary. But for C3s, too valuable to be so casually discarded? Particularly for *double* C3s? It was unheard of.

And not simply lease - lease to *Morafer*, so far it could only be reached through the jump relays. Too far to hear each other telepathically, too far for even the dreaming to reach. Her vision blurred as the full reality set in.

She would never see him again.

The tears came then, the trickle quickly bursting into a flood. Kerelle felt as if something inside her was broken, as if all her bones had shattered and could not be made whole. Her sobs were the only sound in the room as they held each other, lost in their own thoughts. Finally she spoke, her whisper heavy with grief.

"I'll always love you, Galhen. Always."

He stilled against her. They'd never said it. Not when they were gawky teenagers exchanging shy glances at the Academy, not when they shared their first time together, not in the decade they'd been the only constant in each others' lives. They'd sent the feeling over their bond, warmth and affection and longing. But love was too dangerous a word to say aloud.

Galhen's arms tightened around her, and she felt his hot tears mingle with her own.

"I love you, Kerelle. And I will never forget you."

EIGHT

"I GUESS THIS IS IT, THEN." *Kerelle fidgeted with her bag, keenly aware that her transport's pre-flight checks were rapidly finishing. She was nearly out of excuses not to be onboard.*

"I guess it is," *Galhen replied with a hint of amusement. Kerelle wanted to take his hand, or better yet, throw her arms around him and hold tight. But they were standing in the middle of the transport dock, and it was daring enough he was here at all. She was hardly the only newly-minted agent, departing from this dock for her first mission, but she was the only one with a friend to see her off. They'd already gotten a few raised eyebrows.*

So she had to settle for sending him a telepathic burst of affection, and hoping she'd kept her anxiety from leaking through. From the slight quirk of his eyebrow, she hadn't.

You're going to do great, Kerelle, *he sent her.* You shouldn't worry. You're ready for everything they can throw at you.

I hope so. *She stopped trying to hide her nervousness.* I...don't want to let anyone down. *She also didn't want to die. Or kill anyone else, really, but there wasn't going to be much choice about that. She wasn't being assigned to the pirate hunters for her negotiating skills.*

You won't. *Galhen sent her another warm pulse of feeling, all reas-*

surance and lifted spirits. And you'll get to see the galaxy! I'm a bit jealous, really. You'll have to write me and tell me what it's like in the stars.

I'm sure you'll get to see at some point. *Kerelle tried to sound encouraging - she wasn't the only one with mixed feelings on what came next, now that they were officially full PsiCorp Agents.* Your hospital residency is only two years - maybe afterward you'll get assigned to the field too.

I hope so. I'll be rather disappointed if I spend my entire life stationed in Tallimau.

"Agent Evandra!" Supervisor Lumeini called across the dock, slight emphasis on Kerelle's new title. "We're ready to depart. Finish up and get to your seat before we're delayed." She was standing by the entrance to the transport, watching Kerelle with a slight frown.

I guess that's my cue then. *Tears burned in her eyes as she gave him a slight wave and started walking back towards Lumeini, as if she had no hesitation to choose the work.* I miss you already, *she sent with a wild burst of emotion. On impulse, she couldn't help adding -* Don't forget about me! And...I promise I'll come back.

He returned the feeling, with a swell of longing that set her eyes threatening to spill over into tears again. I could *never* forget about you. And I promise, I'll always be here.

***

KERELLE PASSED the next week in a blur, disconnected and numb. True to her word the senator's assistant had departed with Galhen the following morning. She'd felt his warmth through their bond gradually fade, until at last his ship hit the jump relay and he was truly gone. They had spent long periods apart before, but this time was different. This time there was no prospect of reunion, no warmth and affection to come home to. Sold away permanently to Morafer was as final a separation as death.

For once she was eager for her leave to end, if only to give her a distraction.

"You in a staring match with that coffee, Evandra?"

Kerelle raised her head at the unexpected address. When she'd come down for breakfast, the PsiCorp residence hall cafe had been blessedly empty. She abruptly realized it had filled up while she was lost in thought, and several heads were turned in her direction.

"She's just wondering who's going to keep her bed warm now that Ambrel's gone."

"Well, sign me up if she's taking volunteers." The pair started snickering. Romlis and Fanacor. It figured. They might be bigger now, but they were still the same assholes they'd been as teenagers. Romlis in particular had always had it out for her - he was a hard C2, and apparently he'd been the top telekinetic in their cohort before she'd transferred in from Hasha. He'd never quite gotten over that Kerelle could throw more force than he could.

Kerelle met his eyes coolly, then deliberately turned her gaze back to her cup, pointedly ignoring him as she took a sip of now-tepid coffee. Romlis and Fanacor weren't telepaths, but she still ratcheted up her always-present telepathic shields to ensure that no stray feelings slipped out. There were telepaths in the *rest* of the room, and everyone was still watching; some discreetly, others in open anticipation of entertaining drama. Kerelle was forcefully reminded of the *other* reason she'd never really liked the Tallimau PsiCorp base. It was den of stars-damned vipers.

A tray plunked in front of her, and a young woman followed it, blocking Kerelle's line of sight.

"Sorry I'm late!" she said loudly, her short, unnaturally-bright red hair swishing over her shoulders as she settled into her seat. "It's really great to see you again, Keri! We have so much to catch up on!"

The spell broke; Romlis and Fanacor turned back to their own conversation with parting smirks, and the room's attention ebbed away as it became clear that nothing else interesting would happen. Kerelle suppressed a sigh of relief.

"And this," Mila Elith Bereni announced quietly, leaning across the table to be out of eavesdropping earshot, "is exactly why we're not supposed to get attached. You are a *wreck*, Keri. Even idiots like Romlis can tell."

Despite her exasperated tone, the pyrokinetic's eyes were filled with concern, and Kerelle felt a sudden rush of gratitude. Mila was the closest she had to a friend among the Tallimau PsiCorp, but Kerelle wouldn't have thought they were close enough for Mila to intervene in social situations on her behalf. It felt rather touching that she had.

"It's good to see you, Mila," Kerelle answered, hoping her tone conveyed that she meant it. She too kept her voice soft. "And thank you for helping with him. It's been a...difficult week."

Mila snorted softly. "That time we spent six days under siege on Alkamal before the fleet broke through was a 'difficult week.' And you didn't get all mopey and puffy-eyed when we were running out of food and explosives."

She leaned closer. "Look, I know Galhen was special to you. Everyone did. And I'm really sorry things happened like this. Shit, I'm going to miss him too, and I was only assigned with him once. But you've *got* to pull it together before the Director starts to notice."

Kerelle's head shot up, sudden ice trailing down her spine. "Has he said anything?"

"Not to me. Not to anyone, that I've heard. But Keri *everyone* is noticing." Mila glanced around them as if to emphasize her point. "And they're starting to talk. If the Director gets it in his head that you're unfit for duty..."

Kerelle shivered as her hand went involuntarily to her collar. "That would be...bad," she agreed softly.

Mila widened her eyes slightly in an unspoken *well obviously*. "What you really need is a distraction. Let's go out tonight, Keri. Get drunk, get it all out, go home with some handsome stranger you'll never speak to again, get up the next morning and go on with your life." Her face softened a little, and her aura flared with sympathy. "I know you're upset, but mourning for Galhen won't bring him back, and neither will getting yourself in trouble. All you can do is move forward for *you*."

Kerelle inclined her head in acquiescence. At the very least, the oblivion of hard liquor would be a change from staring at the ceiling in her room.

THE CLUB'S lights cut swathes of neon through the swirling artificial fog, flashing in time to the throbbing bass. A mass of bodies ground and gyrated beneath the mirrored ceiling at the room's center, while smaller groups gathered at the numerous bars like insects circling a lantern. Kerelle took another long swig from her glass and eyed them from her spot on the wall.

It was her second drink already, but despite the buzz beginning to rise in her veins she had no intention of abandoning the wall for the frenetic froth of the dance floor. She'd agreed to the night out to appease Mila, and because intellectually she knew the pyrokinetic was right. She had to move forward, or at least make the *appearance* of moving forward. And if the other PsiCorp really were starting to gossip about her mental state, she needed to make that appearance *fast*.

Once they'd actually arrived, however, it became clear she wasn't going to be doing much besides running up a bar tab. It wasn't that she didn't like to dance; it was that she had always danced in clubs like these pressed against Galhen's lean muscles and narrow hips, delighting in his body against hers and the unspoken *later* promised as they moved together. Her stomach turned at the thought of a stranger's touch.

Kerelle took an almost vicious slurp from her drink, savoring the whiskey's burn. A few more of these and she'd be too sloshed to cry herself to sleep. That would have to count for progress.

She wondered if Galhen had arrived at his new home in Morafer. Would he be working right now? Adapting? Or was he staring into his own glass of whiskey on the other side of the galaxy? Her guts twisted - what if he *wasn't*? What if he had accepted her loss and moved on, as they had been taught all their lives to do? Her treacherous imagination conjured up a vision of Galhen out in that teeming mass of dancers, a smile on his lips and a beautiful stranger in his arms.

Her eyes burned.

Kerelle blinked away the tears and sucked down the rest of the whiskey in a sudden swell of anger. At herself, for thinking it - as if the last ten years hadn't proved that Galhen loved her as deeply as she loved him. At this Senator Dalanva, for buying herself a pretty Class 3 telepath as though he were in the window of a pet shop. But most of all, her anger bubbled against SysTech, against all the multigalactics, against an entire system that permitted the enslavement of people like her.

Oh, they dressed it up in words like "contracts" and "talent acquisition rights," and the PsiCorp certainly lived in material comfort. But when you stripped away the professional-sounding language and the trappings of glamor, SysTech had sold Galhen just as sure as if he'd been in chains.

But no, not chains. Just a slim, attractive alloy band that could murder him for disobedience.

"You're doing this whole *clubbing* thing wrong!" Mila's lightly-slurred exclamation startled Kerelle out of her thoughts. She realized her jaw was clenched, her knuckles white around the empty glass. Kerelle hadn't noticed the younger woman's approach. By the looks of her - and the muscled-but-vacant-looking man with an arm around her swaying shoulders - Mila had long since passed Kerelle up on alcohol consumption, and possibly thrown in a hit or two of ambrosia for good measure.

"Look at you, Keri. Look. At. You. Here we are, surrounded by booze, and people, and *boys*," Mila interrupted herself to briefly fondle her new friend, and Kerelle decided not to comment on her distinction of "boys" and "people." Mila abruptly remembered her thought and continued, gesticulating widely. "We're here, and you're still sitting on the wall looking like some kind of grouchy....grouch-person. Nobody wants to dance with a grouch-person!"

Kerelle quashed her instinctive retort that that was the idea. Slurred nagging and all, Mila meant well. She didn't deserve Kerelle's anger, still sizzling terrible and dangerous in her mind.

"I'll be along soon," she said instead. "I just need another drink." Or three.

Kerelle peeled herself off the wall and stalked towards the bar as Mila once again became distracted with her companion. Maybe another whiskey would tamp down that forbidden fury, still coiling tightly in her guts.

NINE

THE DREAM WAS EMPTY. She'd built a warm and cheery setting, a sunny loft apartment overlooking a seaside city. Bright sunlight streamed in through the large windows, highlighting the elegant, modern furnishings. It was exactly the sort of place she'd always fantasized about owning with Galhen, in an alternate world where such a thing was possible. In her secret heart, she'd liked to imagine leisurely walks home along the beachfront, sophisticated meals in the sleek kitchen, late nights relaxing on the balcony watching the summer stars. Maybe even a dog, curled asleep between them as they read in bed.

It seemed so very lonely without Galhen himself.

Kerelle paced the hardwood floor, finally resting her arm against the window. She didn't know what she was expecting - that somehow he would hear her, galaxies away? She already knew their range didn't extend that far. She already knew he wouldn't be here. For some reason *she* was here anyway. Maybe it was because any connection to Galhen, no matter how tenuous, lit a brief glow of warmth in the cold ache of her heart.

When she put it that way, it sounded rather pathetic. So

what if it was. As coping mechanisms went, at least it was harmless.

Kerelle got herself a brightly-patterned teacup down from the minimalist cabinet and took a seat at the dining table, beside the floor-to-ceiling window with a view of the sea. She willed the tea kettle into existence with a thought, and poured herself a steaming cup, sipping it absentmindedly as she admired the view. Another thought and the fluffy dog appeared at her feet, pointed ears laid back as it dozed on the floor. She closed her eyes briefly and concentrated. When she opened them again, Galhen sat in the chair beside hers, clasping his own bright teacup.

It wasn't him, of course, any more than a photo was. The Galhen sitting next to her was a figment of her memory and imagination, a slightly more animated part of the dream scenery. Part of her felt better anyway just seeing him beside her, even knowing it was a simple illusion. Part of her felt worse.

The dream-Galhen smiled at her, painfully like the real thing. Kerelle sighed deeply and twined her fingers with his. Her chest hurt as she looked around the pretty lie she'd built for herself, to keep the truth at bay just a little longer. She lifted their knotted fingers and kissed them, and ended the dream.

Her pillow was still wet with tears when she woke.

CLUBBING MAY HAVE BEEN A BUST, but Mila was not one to give up easily. A few days later, the young pyrokinetic rallied to try again: this time, shopping.

"You need to *care* for yourself," she chirped brightly. "And the best kind of therapy is *retail* therapy!"

Mila might be small and sunny, but sometimes there was no arguing with her. And so before Kerelle could muster an objection, she found herself on the broad, welcoming streets of one of Tallimau's premier shopping districts.

In its way, Lystria Street was a wonderland of fashion. Its eponymous boulevard was lined with gleaming storefronts, many of them flagships for the galaxy's leading luxury brands. Nestled in the smaller streets that branched around it were boutiques for rising fashion houses, their carefully curated selection offering as much a lifestyle vision as a clothing line.

Tourists visiting Tallimau from across the galaxy came here to gawk and window-shop, and back in her Academy days a Lystria Street shopping trip had been a treasured reward. It was the sort of place you could explore for hours, and spend thousands of credits in the blink of an eye. Kerelle had done both in the past, but today Lystria Street's sparkle seemed faint and flat, and the magic that usually drew her in was absent. Instead she found herself simply drifting after Mila as she led them from shop to shop - though the pyrokinetic seemed determined to muster enough enthusiasm for both of them.

"Look!" she cried, grabbing Kerelle's hand and pointing across the street. "Ancharalan has their fall collection in! Let's go look, I know you love their pieces, and you always look *so* good in them!"

Kerelle let herself be practically dragged inside. Mila wasn't wrong, Ancharalan *was* one of her favorite brands, and she *did* look good in their designs. The dress she'd been wearing at the last year-end gala, when Galhen told her she was so beautiful he could hardly breathe, had been one of theirs.

Anything she bought here today, he'd never see her wear. What even was the point?

She tried anyway, forcing herself to pay attention as she wandered the displays. Kerelle might not feel much interest in fashion at the moment, but the fashion itself was never the point. They were here because shopping was a favorite PsiCorp pick-me-up, and despite her malaise Kerelle could recognize that Mila was trying to help her the only way she knew how.

Effectiveness aside, Kerelle deeply appreciated the attempt. Compassion and kindness were not virtues instilled in the PsiCorp.

And so she half-heartedly tried on a series of well-tailored shirts and coats, and let Mila exclaim over how perfect they looked on her, and did her best to pretend she cared as well. She finally selected a few shirts nearly at random, and a dark, structured jacket that even *she* had to admit was quite striking. As she flashed her card at the purchase kiosk, however, Kerelle felt a momentary chill.

She'd never really thought about money. She'd never had to. She wasn't paid, naturally, none of the PsiCorp were, but their company-issued payment cards didn't have a spending limit. Her whole life - or at least, her whole life since she'd left the Academy a full-fledged PsiCorp agent - Kerelle had been able to simply buy whatever she wanted. SysTech's generosity towards its valued agents was one of the perks of service.

But what that also meant, she realized abruptly, was that SysTech could take away all her monetary resources with the click of a few keys.

Intellectually perhaps, she'd always known that SysTech could cut off her funds if she stepped out of line, but it had never really hit home - possibly because stepping out of line never seemed like a possibility. But in the context of her dangerous, insubordinate musings the other night, it seemed painfully obvious that the situation was intentional. It was a method of control, dressed up as a perk. As if the collars weren't enough.

Mila rung up an impressive haul at the kiosk beside her, oblivious to Kerelle's dark thoughts.

"Oh, I'm so glad you decided on that jacket!" she exclaimed, giving Kerelle's small pile a determinedly enthusiastic once-over. "It'll be such a great piece to have once it starts getting colder!"

Kerelle tried to respond with the appropriate noises of agree-ment - and to keep her disquieting thoughts from spilling onto her face. Judging by Mila's expression, she hadn't been terribly successful.

The pyrokinetic gave a barely perceptible sigh before bright-ening again. "It's still early - let's catch a movie before we head back!"

MILA CHOSE the current popular favorite, some sort of quasi-historical romance, and it was not exactly Kerelle's cup of tea. Regardless, she found herself settled in to watch the trials and travails of a beautiful, spirited heiress, robbed of her fortune by fate (and her father's secret gambling problem, though the film seemed to place the blame for this on fate as well). Desperate and alone, the fallen heiress had no choice but to sell her remaining possessions for passage to a new life in the frontier colonies, where the promotional posters had made it clear she would soon meet a handsome lawman.

Kerelle was only half-watching as camera went close on the heroine's face, bravely fighting back tears as she sold her prized possession, a jeweled heirloom necklace from her mother. The music swelled with feeling at the letting go of her past, or some-thing, and the camera lingered on the sparkling jewels disap-pearing into the merchant's closed drawer in case anyone might have missed the cue from the music that this was *symbolic*. But then the heroine stoically pocketed her proceeds, and a sudden thought made Kerelle sit straight up.

Not that she was *really* considering any sort of insubordina-tion, and certainly not considering any sort of *escape*. That was madness, and impossible. But... if she ever went mad and *did* think of considering something like that, she would need funds. SysTech could cut off her payment card at any time, but anything she owned with high resale value could potentially be converted into money. Particularly if those high-resale items were small and easy to carry with her.

She was still mulling that as they left the theater, Mila gushing at how very *romantic* it all had been. She nodded along, and on impulse -

"Her necklace was lovely, wasn't it? Makes me want one like it. Want to stop on the way back and see what they have?"

Mila's immediate, enthusiastic assent pricked Kerelle with guilt at using her friend's magpie nature, but she didn't call off the side trip. A half-hour later they both walked out of the jewelry shop with very beautiful, very expensive pendants.

Mila chattered excitedly about their new acquisitions and Kerelle's guilt intensified - she knew that at least part of the pyrokinetic's over-the-top enthusiasm was because she took Kerelle's renewed interest in shopping as an indication that she was feeling better. She was also feeling wildly subversive. True, she had no plans to *actually* use the jewelry for anything that would get her in trouble. But she'd thought about it, and that thought was the reason she'd bought it.

That felt dangerous enough.

IT STILL FELT dangerous the next day, and Kerelle needed time to think. She made her way to the base gym and, safely installed on a treadmill with her neon blue headphones as a visible do-not-disturb, finally gave her seditious mind free reign.

What if she *did* try to leave? That was easy. If she tried to leave they'd kill her before she'd gotten a meter out the door - or make her wish they had.

That was the entire point of the collars. And while collar activation was a rare, serious punishment, it wasn't an empty threat. There had been a brash boy in her cohort at the Academy who'd tried to desert when they were eighteen, under the theory that the collars were an elaborate ruse concocted to keep them in line. He hadn't made it far before the "ruse" kicked in, and his screams had echoed all the way into the dorms. Kerelle halfway suspected security had dragged him back that way by design.

But assume she *was* able to find a way around the collars. What then? Where would she *go*? Would she find Galhen? Would he even want to escape with her if she did?

Fueled by anxiety she unconsciously picked up her pace, prompting a soft beep of protest from the treadmill as it adjusted its speed to match her. How *was* Galhen doing on Morafer? She knew he must miss her also, but was he happy otherwise? He'd spent ten years in the field with SysTech, and a lot of the work had been hard. Elekar, especially, had been a terrible assignment. Working as a senator's aide sounded comparatively plush. Reliable electricity and running water, no long marches from one camp to the next, low probability of anyone stumbling into his office covered in blood. Maybe he was enjoying it and would be perfectly pleased to stay.

But no - soft and easy was never her Galhen. He was always eager for more to do, more to learn, another mountain to climb. Her mind went back to their conversation on Elekar, how he'd argued that they were lucky to be class-3 and damn the cost. That despite the difficulty class-3 meant *freedom,* or the closest to it that anyone in the PsiCorp could hope for, and some measure of agency within your own life. *At least,* she thought bitterly, *until some rich politician wants to outdo her peers, and takes a liking to your pretty eyes.*

The treadmill beeped. She'd sped up again.

If she were able to build up the funds to escape, and *if* she somehow found a way to overcome the collar, what would she even *do*? The PsiCorp was the only life she'd ever known. SysTech was her jailer, but also her provider - missions might get rough sometimes, but in her day-to-day life she'd never known want. How would she make her way in the universe?

And one thing *was* certain. If she truly did escape, if she proved it truly could be done, they would never stop hunting her.

TEN

A FEW DAYS LATER, she was on her way to the cafe when a message popped up.

Evandra,

Would like to meet briefly this afternoon. Please be at my office at 13:00.

Cafora

Her stomach dropped.

Did he know what she'd been thinking? Did he suspect? Did one of the other telepaths read it off her?

Steady, Kerelle. She took a deep, and focusing breath. There was no way he could know. She hadn't let her shields down since she'd arrived back on Tallimau - she never did, not living in close proximity to a dozen or more fellow telepaths, many of whom had a penchant for vicious gossip. She was also the only C3 telepath currently at the base; none of the others present were strong enough to get through her shields, especially not undetected. It must be about something else. Maybe she was being assigned to a complex new mission.

Maybe she'd been sold too.

Steady. There was no point in speculating what the meeting was about, she had to attend and she'd find out when she got there. What she *could* do was be strategic about how she presented herself.

Back in the safety of her suite, Kerelle laid out her new jewelry collection with a critical eye. She'd acquired several new pieces since the original necklace she bought with Mila; if that had somehow aroused his suspicions then covering it up would only look worse. After a moment's thought, she selected a ring and a large pendant. Both were statement pieces, and they'd been among the most expensive.

She waded next into her closet, deceptively full of clothing that had caught her eye on random shopping trips. In practice, she'd hardly worn any of it; she spent little enough time on Tallimau, and there was no place for bright blouses and carefree skirts on her field missions. Kerelle wasn't entirely sure why she'd bought most of this in the first place. Maybe she'd been caught up in the lifestyle dreams that Lystria Street peddled, as if clean lines and a chic silhouette could redeem her from the battlefield.

As it was, the closet always felt like it belonged to someone else.

Near the back, she found a lightweight blouse with a scooped neckline that was perfect. Kerelle slipped it on and added her jewelry, and gave her reflection a quick once-over. The understated shirt drew attention to her large, intricate necklace, and both were complemented by the sparkling ring. She looked nothing at all like a woman who felt guilty for her recent purchases; rather, she looked like someone with an appreciation for status and luxury. Most importantly, she looked like she *cared*.

Kerelle couldn't help the satisfied smile that curved her lips. She might not be particularly *good* at fashion, exactly, not the way that Galhen was, but she did clean up nice.

All right, then. There was no way anyone could have read her thoughts, and if Cafora somehow suspected what sparked her sudden interest in fine jewelry, then her clothing proclaimed that she had nothing to hide. She'd also done some light research when she started to grow her collection, and if prompted Kerelle was reasonably certain she could prattle off enough trivia to pass as a gemology dilettante. That should count as a plus, if Cafora asked. Growing up in the PsiCorp, she'd been practically *conditioned* to bury negative feelings in material excess. Surely cheering herself up with an expensive hobby would count as proof she was toeing the line.

Really though, there was no reason for Cafora to even be suspicious in the first place. If anything gave her away, it was going to be her own nervousness.

Steady.

Cafora greeted her knock almost immediately. The Tallimau PsiCorp Director was a pleasant-looking man, his face still mostly unlined despite dark hair mostly gone to steel, contrasting against the bright silver of his customary psiblocker. He ushered her into his immaculate office with a paternal smile.

He wore that smile more often than not, and from Kerelle's experience he had earned his reputation for being measured and fair with his charges. Still, she had never been quite able to warm to him, and even after a decade and a half in his organization, being the object of his attention was unnerving.

Knowing he had complete discretion to flip her collar on was probably a big part of that.

Cafora gestured for her to sit as he closed the door. She did, politely declining his offer of tea and trying to school her face into pleasant, professional neutrality.

"You wanted to see me, sir?" She kept her voice light and unconcerned; it wouldn't do to look overly eager. "Is there an issue with my report from Elekar?"

She knew damn well there wasn't, but might as well get the innocent explanation out there now.

"No, your work was excellent, as usual. I've made a note to the division head that you were instrumental in the success of our operations there." Cafora paused and folded his hands on his desk, giving her a kind smile. "I actually wanted to talk about you, Kerelle. Are you feeling all right?"

His tone was solicitous, but red flags shot up immediately. The only reason anyone in SysTech management might give a damn about her feelings would be if they thought she might allow the dreaded *personal issues* to affect her work. She needed to play this very carefully.

"I'm fine, sir, thank you for asking." She tried to sound idly curious why he was asking - and certainly not defensive.

"Are you sure?" The kind smile was back, and his voice was gentle, as if to invite confidences. As if she would be foolish enough to offer any; believing that management was on your side was junior-agent delusion. "Sometimes I find that even little issues can grow over time to become big issues, if we ignore them."

He rested his hands on his desk and leaned in slightly. "You're very important to the organization, Kerelle, and I would hate for you to face a problem that could have been avoided if it were dealt with earlier. That's why I thought it might be best for us to have a check-in, to make sure you were doing well."

Chills ran down her spine but Kerelle kept her face pleasantly neutral through sheer force of will.

"Your concern means a lot, sir," she forced herself to smile. "Thank you. I *am* fine, though - really."

He inclined his head slightly. "I'm glad to hear that. Some of your fellow agents mentioned how concerned they were for you."

She tried to look surprised. "Oh?"

"I heard you were very upset about Agent Ambrel's departure." Shit, there it was. Ten credits said it was Romlis, that slimy asshole. She should have known he wouldn't just leave it alone.

Steady. Best lie is a grain of truth. She thought fast.

"Oh." Kerelle slid her eyes away, hoping she looked suitably embarrassed. "I was, I guess - we had some good times. Plus we were supposed to go to a resort on Aulayie together after we got back from Elekar, and then he left and I had to cancel. I was kinda down for a few days, but Mila took me shopping and I'm feeling a lot better." She looked back at Cafora, whose face gave nothing away. "I feel bad for making everyone worry, though."

Cafora nodded slowly, apparently accepting her answer. His eyes lingered on her pendant but he did not remark on it.

"Well, I'm certainly glad to hear that your colleague's concerns were overblown," he repeated. "Just always know you can come to us, if you need to talk. I always prefer to prevent issues with my agents, rather than deal with them afterward." He watched her carefully over his warm smile.

Unspoken warning acknowledged and received. She smiled back, channeling the bright-eyed enthusiasm she'd once had as a young agent who believed what she'd been taught. "Thank you, sir, I'll keep that in mind in the future."

He dismissed her after that, and as she made her deliberately casual way down the corridor she was careful that her only sigh of relief was mental. She probably wasn't out of the woods, but she was fairly certain she'd just escaped an official reprimand. This time, anyway - Cafora's intimations about addressing issues before they escalated carried an unmistakable warning that escalation was in the future, if she didn't course-correct now.

All right, strategy. She'd have to make more of an effort to seem normal for the rest of her time on Tallimau, particularly around her fellow agents, who apparently had nothing better to do than try to sabotage her with management. If she was going to risk trouble with their masters, it would be for something damn more effective than moping around.

She just had to buy herself the time to figure out what that something was.

ELEVEN

FOR THE FIRST time in her career, Kerelle was happy to start the routine leading up to the scheduled end of her leave. Usually an upcoming assignment prompted a mix of vague dread that she would likely be given a distasteful task, and dull resignation that she really ought to be used to that by now. But this time? Distasteful or not, almost anything seemed worth a ticket off of Tallimau.

Kerelle had to assume she was being quietly observed at all times, and the entire base had become unbearably stifling as a result. The effort of feigning positivity and interest in the Tallimau social scene was exhausting - particularly once Mila had departed for *her* latest assignment. It was made worse by the fact that she couldn't actually know if it was all paying off, or if management saw straight through her and was simply documenting incidents for a formal reprimand.

At least in the field she could breathe. No one in the Security Force gave two shits about her attitude, as long as she produced explosions on demand.

Standard practice was for agents to undergo a medical examination before returning to field, and so a few days before her reassignment was due Kerelle found herself in a doctor's office, being poked and prodded and tested. It was a routine, no-surprises kind of appointment - she was in excellent health with no areas of concern - and they were winding down when the medic conducting the examination was called out of the room. He apologized for the interruption and hurried out, promising to return quickly. In his haste, he left his tablet sitting unlocked.

Unlocked, and open to the personnel database that listed everything there was to know about individual PsiCorp agents.

Kerelle hesitated a moment, knowing it was confidential and she shouldn't look, and dove for it.

It would not do to be caught with this, and she kept her senses wide open to detect the medic's return. But here was a golden chance to find out how she stood after her interview with Cafora, and she wasn't going to waste it. A few taps took her from the medical files to the general personnel database; she hastily swiped through to the disciplinary records. She breathed a sigh of relief as she didn't see her name among recent activity, but it immediately turned to a gasp as *another* name caught her eye.

Galhen Tarau Ambrel stood out like it was written in blood. Two records, auto-generated, of collar activation for discipline. Both since he'd been sold to Dalanva.

Blood roared in her ears as the shock pounded through her, and for a terrible moment she thought she was going to faint. She almost missed the medic's approaching return, and had to frantically swipe back to the screen he had left it on. She just managed to replace it on the desk and retake her place on the exam table before the doorknob started to turn.

Steady. Steady. Steady. Kerelle fought for normalcy, and if the medic noticed her state, he didn't let on. A few signed forms later and she was cleared for return to active duty in certified good health. She managed to hold it together until she could make it back to her rooms, but as the door locked behind her she collapsed on the bed with a sob.

She could hardly process this. Collar activation? *Twice?* Galhen had never even come *close* to collar activation, not in all the years he served SysTech. Her erstwhile classmate's screams of agony echoed across her memory as her treacherous imagination conjured up Galhen instead. Kerelle felt sick with horror and grief...but as it ran through her mind again and again, rage ignited in her like a gas fire.

Galhen was an *exemplary* agent. He served with distinction and dedication for ten years, without question or complaint. He consistently, obediently handed SysTech successful results. Never in ten years was there a black mark on his record, no hint of any need for discipline, especially not as extreme as the collar.

He was, in short, everything they were taught to be. And look where it got him.

Despite everything he did for SysTech, despite playing by all their rules, despite even his strategic value, Galhen was sold like an object because SysTech saw an opportunity for short term profit. And now there was proof, *proof in their own records!* that this Dalanva woman was harming him, and the company did not care. They already got Galhen's service, they got Dalanva's money, and they didn't care what happened to him now.

There had always been an implicit understanding, she realized, in all their service to SysTech. Disobey us, and you will force our hand to correct you. But do as you're told, and we won't come for you. Dedicate yourself to excellence, follow your orders without question, model the behavior we've taught you, and you will earn comfort and safety.

That "understanding" was a lie, a simulacrum of agency. Disobedience might be punished, but clearly SysTech felt no need to hold up its end of the bargain otherwise.

Kerelle focused on deep, steady breaths, trying to force

herself to calm down. Fury would solve nothing. She needed to be strategic about what to do next. About what it could mean to *escape.*

Escape had always seemed impossible, even to think about. The risk was far too high, the consequences terrible. But in that moment, it became clear as dawn that she really had nothing to lose.

Certainly, she could be killed in a failed attempt. But she'd spent her whole life trying to protect herself by keeping her head down and doing what was asked of her, and what happened to Galhen proved it was no real protection at all. As long as she was owned by SysTech, safety and security were illusions.

She had to get out, or die trying. She'd be careful. She'd be methodical. But she'd find a way.

DESPITE HER NEWFOUND DETERMINATION, Kerelle was no closer to devising an escape plan when she was called in to the assistant director's office for her next assignment briefing. It was not quite what she was expecting.

"Agent Evandra, are you familiar with the dispute around Zharal V?"

It sounded vaguely familiar. "That's the moon with all the biotech labs, isn't it? Wasn't that owned by StellarEye?"

"It was," the other woman confirmed. "You may recall the StellarEye Corporation entered liquidation several years ago following an extended period of decline. Prior to final shutdown StellarEye amassed a substantial amount of debt. SysTech was one of the chief creditors. Consolidated Energy was another."

Assistant Director Jaselt swiped through the briefing documents to pull up an aerial map of a large city.

"The status of Zharal V has been disputed since the liquidation. Our debt negotiations with StellarEye included a provision for transferring ownership of the moon in the event of a default, and we are clearly entitled to Zharal V as part of our settlement, but ConEn is disputing the validity of the documents and keeping the whole thing tied up in court. In the meantime we've landed peacekeeping troops on the moon to protect our interests. Regrettably ConEn has done the same."

Kerelle began to get an inkling of where this was going.

"Naturally tension is considerable on the moon's surface, but thus far both sides have avoided violent conflict. However, we have reason to believe things may be coming to a head."

"And that's where I come in?"

"Precisely, although not in the capacity you may be thinking." The other woman tapped the map and pulled up a closer view of a large, sprawling building. "This is the Prime Zharala convention center. For the last twenty years it's been the site of one of the largest biotechnology conferences in the sector. That conference just commenced this morning, and many of the galaxy's most prominent biotech scientists are there now."

Kerelle raised her eyebrows. "That seems risky with everything going on. Why didn't they move the venue?"

"Prime Zharala is a SysTech property," Jaselt answered shortly. "Factoring in lost revenue and reputational damage from moving the conference, risk/benefit analyses determined that the best course of action was to continue as planned. We expended considerable lobbying resources to keep the conference at its traditional location."

Since they were having this conversation, Kerelle was going to assume those risk/benefit analyses hadn't worked out in reality. *Imagine that.* She said nothing, however, and simply nodded her understanding as Jaselt continued.

"Since then, however, the situation has changed. The judges have indicated they will issue a ruling in the next week, and that it will likely be in our favor. As a result the situation on the ground is escalating. The conference is scheduled to run for another two weeks, but given the circumstances management doesn't want to take the risk. The academics attending are preeminent in their fields, and would make ideal hostages for ConEn to apply pressure on our clients."

Jaselt closed the window for the briefing docs and handed the tablet back to Kerelle. "We're sending an additional security team to manage the evacuation. It will be orderly, and we are not calling it an evacuation. If events take a turn, however, we're counting on both your defensive abilities against a hostile ConEn force and your capability to telepathically locate any potential missing persons. You leave tomorrow morning."

———————

BACK IN HER QUARTERS, Kerelle packed lightly for the mission to Zharal V. If all went well, it would be a brief trip. A small part of her was incredulous that this was happening at all; surely it didn't take a strategic mastermind to see that it was a terrible idea to hold a prominent event in the middle of a standoff. A larger part of her was *not at all* surprised. Gross irresponsibility in pursuit of short-term profit was classic SysTech.

After a moment's hesitation, she carefully wrapped most of her jewelry and tucked it into her pack. She still had no idea how she was going to escape, but if an opportunity happened to arise while she was out in the field she needed to be ready to take it. She debated bringing her entire collection, but she worried that if management had any lingering concerns about her it might arouse suspicion. After a brief debate, she left behind a few of the less valuable pieces to give the impression she intended to return.

Of course, she most likely *would* return, but she wanted to stay optimistic.

The next day she settled in for her flight to Zharal V, and

took the opportunity to page through her mission documents for anything Jaselt might have forgotten to mention. Skimming the list of scientists she was supposed to babysit, Kerelle's eye caught on a name partway down.

Nalea Tarau Ambrel.

TWELVE

KERELLE STEPPED off the transport into an airy port station, complete with bright sun warming her face and mild breeze ruffling her hair. Unlike Tallimau's towering steel-and-glass monoliths, Zharal V's architecture was wide and low-slung, seeming to top out at no more than ten stories. Kerelle almost breathed out a sigh of relief at the sight of the sky, stretching boundlessly out above her.

Or maybe it was just relief to be away from Tallimau once again. She felt as though she'd been let out from a cage, in more ways than one.

The Security Force unit she was to accompany had arrived shortly before her; after a quick round of introductions they set out for the Prime Zharala center with a local guide. It was a pleasant walk through picturesque boulevards, lined with shops and cafes and people going about their business. At first glance, there was nothing to indicate that Zharal V was on the brink of any trouble.

Curious, Kerelle slightly dampened her telepathic shields to let in the psychic ambiance. With a start, she immediately raised them again.

The streets might *look* like everything was normal, but the feelings of the people on them said otherwise. Tight tension bubbled in the thoughts of nearly everyone they passed, a vague dread that forces beyond their control were building towards conflict. Now that she was looking for it, she could hear the almost manic undertone in the aggressively normal chatter that swirled around them - as if by refusing to acknowledge what was happening, the citizenry might keep it at bay.

She realized, too, that her group was moving at a good pace despite the bustling street. The crowds melted away before a group of SysTech uniforms like a school of fish evading a shark.

Another thought struck her then, and she slipped closer to their guide to ask.

"I haven't seen any ConEn colors since we touched down," Kerelle noted quietly. "Is that expected?"

"We *shouldn't* see them, not over here. They stay in their territory, we stay in ours," the guide replied stiffly. "The ConEn base is further east, and they tend to fly in through the other port." She glanced quickly back at Kerelle, as if to assess her likelihood to start trouble. "Don't wander off without me or one of the other locals. We know how to get anywhere you need without crossing paths."

Kerelle could tell the other woman didn't really want to talk about this, but she wanted to know what she was dealing with. She pressed. "Are they close enough that crossing paths is likely?"

Another glance backward, this time lingering on the PsiCorp insignia on her jacket. "They're already closer to Prime Zharala than any of us are comfortable with," her guide admitted finally. "But so far they haven't made any moves. Hopefully when they finally lose their case they'll back off and we can all get back to normal."

Kerelle gave a noncommittal noise of agreement. Hopefully that *would* happen, but management wouldn't have sent Class-3

PsiCorp if they thought it was likely. A storm was coming to Zharal V.

She hoped she would be long gone with the scientists before it hit.

The idea that one of those scientists would be Galhen's sister hovered constantly at the back of her mind. Kerelle hadn't quite figured out the significance of that; there was a part of her that wanted to introduce herself, though she had no idea what she'd say if she did. The whole idea felt completely surreal - that *she* might meet Nalea, but Galhen never would.

———

"CANCEL? Right now, just out of the blue? Do you have any *idea* how much went into planning this conference?"

When they'd arrived at the event and quietly pulled the conference chair aside to explain the situation, Kerelle had anticipated that he would quickly cooperate and help them get things underway. From the steadily rising timbre of his voice - not to mention the red in his face - that had been a highly inaccurate assumption.

The squad leader Captain Teresit kept his voice level, though Kerelle could sense his growing irritation. Apparently he hadn't been expecting it to be this difficult either. "We are aware of the inconvenience, Dr. Bolendy - "

"Inconvenience? I have hundreds of very busy people who took time out of their responsibilities to come to this event, nearly two dozen panelists whose travel arrangements were paid for by the conference, several joint experiments being conducted as we speak - this is an outrage, not an *inconvenience*. We were *specifically* and *repeatedly* assured that SysTech security would be more than sufficient. If that was not the case, then why was the conference held here at all?"

Dr. Bolendy continued on his incensed tirade, but his

projected thoughts told a different story. Kerelle could clearly sense his considerable anxiety - the chair wasn't stupid, he could tell the situation was deteriorating as much as anyone. But he was also not terribly keen to march off with a heavily-armed SysTech squad that could just as easily take the scientists hostage themselves. Well, she couldn't blame him for that one. She wouldn't be entirely surprised if that were buried in one of the backup plans.

Some of Captain Teresit's annoyance had bled through into his expression, and he gave Kerelle a significant glance. Assistance please.

She gave him a slight nod and lightly reached out to Bolendy's mind. She only wanted a small telepathic nudge - just to push his fear of being caught between the two multigalactics higher than his discomfort at going with the SysTech team.

Midsentence, Bolendy paled. "Yes...well...I...It's certainly unfortunate, but given the circumstances I can see why the evacuation is necessary. I can help you gather the others." He'd started sweating profusely, and his fear was almost palpable.

Kerelle belatedly realized she might have nudged a bit harder than intended, and she felt a faint blush blooming on her cheeks. She'd never quite had Galhen's deft hand at telepathic encouragement.

She briefly considered trying to calm him, but decided against it - she might overshoot again, and at least this way he had a sense of urgency. All the same, she sensed a wave of unease from the squad as they watched the stammering professor gather his papers. They knew what she'd done, and they didn't like to be reminded that she could do it.

Well, the sooner they all got out of here, the sooner they didn't need to be reminded of it at all.

Even with Bolendy's help, rounding up the rest of the conference was like herding cats. Everyone attending seemed to have valuable research they couldn't leave behind, or an experiment in progress that was *almost finished* and simply needed another two hours, couldn't they wait? Kerelle had to give several more nudges as they worked their way through the group, though she was careful to be more gentle. Slowly and painfully things came together, and soon they had a growing crowd of people and materials assembled in the lobby.

Captain Teresit didn't seem assured by their progress, however. In fact, he grew visibly more agitated as the process dragged on. Kerelle watched him closely as he gesticulated angrily at a recalcitrant scientist. He hadn't said anything, but...

Shamelessly, she read his mind. She didn't have to try very hard, it was bubbling right there at the surface, growing in intensity with each passing minute. He'd gotten word shortly after they landed this morning: a ConEn fleet was moving to blockade Zharal V. Their group needed to get out immediately, or they wouldn't be able to get out at all.

She pulled back in dismay, trying to keep her face neutral as she processed this development, and the fact that *of course*, she *hadn't been informed*. A sudden shout from Bolendy cut through her thoughts.

"We're missing people! Several top delegates left this morning for some field tests, and they were supposed to return over an hour ago. I just learned they never arrived back." He wrung his hands and looked pleadingly at them. "You have to go find them before we can evacuate!"

Whether the captain intended to send out a search party or cut and run with the scientists they *did* have, Kerelle would never know. As he opened his mouth to reply, his words were lost in a sudden deafening boom that shook the building.

The assembled civilians started to scream and Kerelle hurriedly tossed up a shield against any falling debris. Just in time, too - another great boom sounded, closer this time. The force of the second bomb shattered the conference hall's tall windows, spraying debris and broken glass against her barriers. Through the chaos, Kerelle could make out the roar of aircraft above.

It was too late to evacuate. The ConEn fleet was already here.

THIRTEEN

PANDEMONIUM ERUPTED IMMEDIATELY. The scientists began to panic en masse, the steadier ones casting around for something to crawl under while others simply screamed in place. Another terrible boom rocked the building, and the smell of smoke seeped in through the broken windows. Somewhere in the city was burning, probably several somewheres.

So much for the quiet escape.

To his credit, Captain Teresit kept his head, immediately rallying his squad to get the scientists to the basement. It was soon apparent that Bolendy would be no use; the conference chair seemed to be having a minor breakdown. Several of the others weren't far from it, and every time the building shook a fresh wave of panic swept through their charges. Kerelle couldn't blame them, but it wasn't helping.

"Up, you have to get up, we have to get to the basement!" The captain struggled to be heard over the din. "It's not safe here, we have to get below ground!"

Another blast hit, this time accompanied by a concussive force that threw everyone off their feet. An ominous creak sounded overhead; one of the fanciful artworks suspended from the ceiling broke free with a terrifying *crack* and plummeted down. Swearing, Kerelle managed to grab it telekinetically, its heavy metal frame halting centimeters from Bolendy's prone, trembling form. With a grunt she flung it aside, shattering it with a terrible crash against the ruined faux-marble floors.

"Basement," she growled. "Now."

What the shuddering walls and shouting soldiers had failed to do, a splash of showy telekinesis accomplished. The group began to run.

Kerelle ran with them, an uneasy eye on the ceilings. It seemed unlikely that ConEn would directly bomb the conference site - angering virtually every major biotech research facility in the galaxy would be bad for business. Things could get out of hand, though, especially in a bombing run, and you never knew. If ConEn leadership was as short-sighted as SysTech, all bets were off.

Kerelle tried to help by projecting psychic calm over the group to help herd them downstairs, though it was a challenge when she wasn't exactly the picture of serenity herself. Burning *stars*, but she wished Galhen were here. He'd have them all walking downstairs single file without breaking a sweat.

Panic nearly enveloped the group again when they reached the basement to find the doors locked. Kerelle unceremoniously ripped them from their hinges, and shoved the closest scientists inside. The others crowded in soon after.

By the looks of things, the cavernous basement was where Zharala Prime's maintenance and cleaning staff stored their tools. The scientists huddled in the basement's dim light amidst mops and buckets, while muffled blasts continued to echo from above. Kerelle didn't want to say anything, but it seemed like the bombs had been dropping for a long time - longer than she would've expected, if the goal was to hamstring the SysTech group. A sick question curled in the back of her mind; had

ConEn lost their case, and decided that if they couldn't have the moon then no one could?

His charges secured for the moment, Captain Teresit had posted up at the edge of the group, trying to raise the main SysTech base on comms. His only answer was a crackling silence. The squad had held discipline well throughout the evacuation, but nervous mutters began to rise among them, woven into projected thoughts and fears that swirled at the edge of Kerelle's mind. *Trapped down here - no way off - the whole base dead -*

She shook her head almost violently to clear it, shoving her own fears down. They needed to get some answers, and they needed them soon. If the base wasn't answering, there were other ways.

Kerelle took a seat on the ground beside the captain and stretched out with her senses. The SysTech presence here was significant, she couldn't be the only PsiCorp on the moon. She had a moment's regret they hadn't swung by the main base earlier - it was always easier to find someone when you knew who you were looking for. Still, they were likely looking too. She cast her thoughts in the direction of the local base.

Jackpot. Kerelle brushed another startled telepath, who latched on to her like Kerelle was a lifeboat in a stormy sea.

Oh thank the stars, someone's out there. This is Agent Parhet, C1 telepath, field aide to Commander Harsing of Demela Base. What's your status and position?

Kerelle gestured to get Teresit's attention. "I've got contact with the base commander's PsiCorp aide." He nodded grimly and moved closer.

"Can they tell us what in the void is going on out there?" He kept his voice low - though judging from the glances they were getting from their charges, the scientists had already figured out this wasn't going well.

This is Agent Evandra, C3 telepath, C3 telekinetic, assisting with the Zharala Prime evacuation. We were gathering the civilians when the bombs hit, currently sheltering in the conference center's basement level. What's your status? We haven't been able to raise the base on comms.

That's because comms are all down. We took several direct hits. It's pretty obvious Demela Base was one of their main targets. He sounded frustrated. *Fortunately our alarms did their job, and the majority of personnel were able to evacuate to the fortified sublevel.* She caught a subcurrent of bitter laugh. *So we're cowering in a basement right now as well.*

Kerelle relayed the conversation to the captain. His frown deepened, but he didn't look surprised. She held up a quick hand as he opened his mouth; Parhet was talking again.

Commander Harsing relays her gratitude that you're alive, and that we need any assistance you can provide. Most of the base is rubble, including our local aircraft - which means we can't chase down those bombers, which means we're at ConEn's mercy until they decide they're bored of dropping bombs on us.

Parhet paused briefly as if listening - probably to this Commander Harsing. *There's a planetary defense system with some surprisingly high-end anti-aircraft cannons. It's controlled from the ground, and it'll give us a chance against the bombers. We're pinned down here, but we need someone to get there and take control of it.*

Kerelle passed the information on, wondering with a shade of irritation why they didn't *already* have people stationed there. It had been a rhetorical question, but Parhet answered it anyway.

We did. They sure don't seem to be there now.

An image quickly appeared in her mind - the defense system building, overlaid by its map coordinates. *You're not completely alone on this. We had a secondary team away when the bombs hit, and I've had intermittent contact with their C2 telepath attache. It sounds like they're under heavy fire but working their way toward the defense system. Harsing wants you both to rendezvous there if possible, take the defenses, help us start getting this shitshow turned around. Expect heavy action all the way in. You on it?*

Yes, Kerelle sent as she conveyed the plan and the captain nodded his understanding. *See you at the cannons.*

OBVIOUSLY THE SCIENTISTS couldn't come along on this endeavor, and so in short order the captain had split their force. A small team would stay behind to ensure the scientists' safety in the basement, while the majority - and Kerelle - set out for the defenses. The stay team were clearly unhappy to be left with no means of communication, but there was nothing for it. Given how hot things were likely to get, Kerelle could hardly stay behind as a glorified comm system.

They proceeded cautiously up the dim stairs to the main floor of the ruined conference center. The building was a mess, but largely intact. Her earlier instinct had been right - ConEn was avoiding scientist casualties.

The rest of the city was not so lucky. They emerged into a nightmarish scene of rubble and flames, the city blocks rendered unrecognizable but for scattered bits of signage and architecture. From the looks of it, the downtown area had been specifically targeted. Kerelle had to wonder if the real objective had been to isolate Zharala Prime.

Anger coiled in her gut as they passed further into the wrecked streets. Hours ago this had been a bustling civilian hub. Now it was ash and debris, and who knew how many lives were destroyed - all because SysTech and ConEn were in a pissing match. The sheer callousness of it all was staggering.

Kerelle clenched her teeth and fought the emotion down. She couldn't think about any of this right now - she needed to focus on staying alive. She could feel after they'd gotten to safety.

As if on cue, shots rang out ahead of them, and one of the soldiers ahead of her staggered back with a grunt. The squad immediately formed up as the captain shouted orders, just as numerous shapes wearing ConEn crimson emerged from the smoke.

His words were drowned out as the SysTech team returned fire in sharp, percussive bursts, but Kerelle needed no instructions. Enclosing herself in a quick shield, she wrapped her telekinetics around the closest person in red and flung them hard against the outer wall of a ruined cafe, a sickening crack confirming they wouldn't get up. Shouts of *PsiCorp!* spread among the ConEn group like flames through dry tinder.

Kerelle didn't wait for them to react; she grabbed another two, dashing them against the rubble. Soft pops rippled against her shield - they were aiming for *her* now.

Let them.

She began hurling chunks of debris into the ConEn group, scattering the line into the waiting fire of the SysTech squad. ConEn faltered almost immediately, their fear curling up at her senses. They hadn't expected PsiCorp out here, knew their numbers were far too low to fight her. The ConEn leader made a weak show of trying to rally, then the survivors went into full retreat.

The SysTech team didn't follow; there was nothing to be gained by chasing down ConEn fighters, not when bombs still shook the city around them. Instead they regrouped to push on towards the cannons. Kerelle expanded her shields to encompass the squad, anticipating the inevitable next attack.

They didn't have to wait long. Scarcely two blocks from the last ambush site, a hail of bullets bounced off her shields and clattered to the broken street. The SysTech squad formed up, and once again Kerelle found herself flinging deadly force against anyone in red. This group was better prepared than the last - they struck in a loose formation and retreated back in orderly fashion, melting back into the hazy streets. The word had gotten out that there were PsiCorp with the SysTech team, and Kerelle suspected ConEn had shifted its strategy to attrition.

Still, that gave SysTech an opportunity to do the same. Every red-clad body they stepped over now was one fewer they would have to deal with at the cannons. She grimly reformed the shield as the advance resumed.

They had to fight for every centimeter to the planetary defense. There were far more ConEn troops on the ground than intel had suggested, and they were clearly arrayed to defend the cannons. It became a deadly game of strike and advance, retreat and regroup, as the SysTech squad fought steadily forward.

This was not, Kerelle reflected angrily as she caught her breath between attacks, a spontaneous reaction to a legal setback. Not this many troops, not this well-ordered. Not the almost surgical strike on Demela Base. It was painfully obvious that ConEn had been planning this for quite some time, and just as obvious that SysTech had grossly underestimated their opponent.

Once again, the company's idiocy was being paid for in blood.

The silhouette of the defense cannons drew closer and closer on the horizon. Finally they had clear line-of-sight on the building's facade. As they drove off the latest ConEn attack, Captain Teresit gave the orders to advance on the doors.

Almost as soon as he'd said it, a stack of rubble suddenly exploded, sending SysTech personnel flying. Kerelle whipped her head around to locate the new threat, and tightened her shields. That hadn't been a bomb; that was a telekinetic blast.

ConEn's PsiCorp had come to play.

———————

TWO THINGS BECAME apparent almost immediately: the ConEn psionics weren't nearly as powerful as Kerelle, and there were more of them than of her. How *many* more, she wasn't sure, but the coordinated burst of small explosions surrounding her squad argued there were at least two of them. And they weren't alone - red-clad figures popped out from the battered buildings that lined the street, guns at the ready.

Kerelle threw up a broad shield around the squad; it was a larger area than she could usually cover effectively, but she hoped to deflect at least some of the incoming bullets and debris. Screams from behind her indicated she hadn't been completely successful, but as the squad fanned out around her it seemed mostly intact. At least it seemed they had been trained to fight psionics; the soldiers scattered into loose formation to present smaller targets without needing to be told.

Kerelle threw more of her energy behind the shield, trusting it to hold for the moment, and glanced around quickly for Captain Teresit.

"I'll engage," she called at him. "Focus the squad on defense, and picking off the mundanes. If you get a shot at their PsiCorp, take it." He nodded tightly and relayed orders. Kerelle shifted her attention back to the attackers.

The ConEn soldiers had them surrounded now, their bullets a series of rapid-fire *pops* against her shield. First things first - she couldn't focus on the other psionics while she was shielding the whole squad, and she couldn't lower that shield while they were under a hail of active fire. A sharp telekinetic blow struck against the shield then, and another from a different direction. The ConEn PsiCorp might be weaker psionics than her, but if they could keep the SysTech team pinned down without cover like this, they'd get through her shields eventually.

Time to sort that out, then.

Kerelle took a deep, deliberative breath, drawing in her power as she drew air in her lungs. She held it for an instant, just long enough to confirm ConEn's positioning. Then all the force she'd gathered, she expelled just as quickly, sending a shockwave flooding outward from their shield with concussive force.

All around them the ConEn squad was thrown off their feet, some sprawled in graceless heaps, others tossed like dolls against obstacles behind them. Kerelle gave Teresit the shields-down sign, and shrank her defenses to just herself. The sharp stacatto of SysTech returning fire started up in her ears as she scanned the battlefield for the other psionics.

They certainly had a bead on *her*. Another sharp blow against her shield, and dull *crack* as a loose chunk of concrete smashed against the barrier and skittered down the ground in pieces. They'd been aiming for her head with that one; if the shield had faltered she'd be dead. She shoved the thought down and rein-forced her defenses, finishing her visual sweep. She couldn't ID any of those red uniforms as PsiCorp; no matter. Time to put that double-C3 to use.

First, though, she needed to get them off her.

Kerelle raked her telekinetics along the pockmarked street, sluicing up bits of shrapnel and debris like some kind of perverse fishing net. She flung it down again with hurtling force, sending screams through the ConEn ranks. The telekinetic strikes against her shields suddenly halted - as she'd hoped, the other PsiCorp were distracted with their own defense.

She grabbed the opportunity and quested out with her senses, quickly scanning the minds around her. There, in the sea of mundanes - a class-1 telekinetic. She could only sense the one; the other must be a multitalent as well, capable of shielding their presence. The C1, however, obviously could not. Her psychic signature was clearly discernible from where she crouched behind a half-fallen wall.

Kerelle lashed out and snapped her neck before she even realized it. One down.

An external wave of fury radiated across the battlefield, battering her senses like a weapon in itself. The other ConEn

PsiCorp, then - a telepath/telekinetic like her, though not a class-3. She strengthened her mental defenses again and the feeling receded, though she could still sense his emotional firestorm like a distant heat. The C1 had been more than a friend.

There was no hiding now. The surviving ConEn psionic stepped out to face her, jagged shrapnel swirling around him at the ready. She gathered her own weapons and stared him down.

He was not as powerful as her, but he was well-trained, and his fury lent him strength. They fought back and forth then, hurling bits of the broken world around them with deadly force and pushing down with waves of concussive energy, trying to strike through each others' shields. Kerelle found herself breathing heavily from the effort, and knew her opponent must be feeling the same.

Finally she saw her opening - he dodged a hail of stones hurtling like bullets, and she felt his shield falter. Before he could recover she brought down a hard telekinetic shove from above him. He staggered, and she struck again before he could regain his footing, pinning him to the ground. He tried to push back, as her power bore down like an invisible wall, but in the end she was simply stronger. His shield cracked beneath the sheer weight of force against it. It was over in an instant.

The field was utterly silent, and Kerelle belatedly realized the mundane soldiers had all withdrawn to cover while the psionics dueled. She didn't sense any ConEn troops nearby; they must have retreated when their PsiCorp fell. Her own squad cautiously emerged from their cover. They eyed her warily, like one might watch a dangerous animal.

She couldn't blame them. There was no thrill of victory rising in her veins; instead, a hollow sort of sadness spread out from her chest, as she stood over the body of another psionic who'd never had any more choice in his life than she had. Who'd cared for the other telekinetic, enough that her death had made him reckless with grief. She wished she'd never crossed paths with either of them.

Maybe a dangerous animal was what she *was*.

"Agent?" Teresit's voice broke through her dark thoughts. Kerelle took a shuddering breath and turned to face him, wrestling down her reaction to the battle. *Feel later*. Survive now.

"Ready to proceed, captain," she acknowledged. He gave her a tight nod and reformed the squad. The way to the cannons was clear.

After that, it was no great challenge to take the guns. The bulk of ConEn's force had apparently been focused on keeping them from reaching the objective, and once Kerelle blew open the barricaded doors they met only token resistance. In no time at all, they'd secured the building and set up a gunner crew.

Despite it all, Kerelle couldn't deny a burst of savage satisfaction at the first booming report of the anti-aircraft gun, and flaming ship that streaked the sky immediately after. The bombs over Zharal V finally went silent.

Parhet was relieved to hear of their success, and a few hours later they were joined by the survivors of Demela Base. The secondary defense squad he'd mentioned soon joined them as well, battered but largely intact. The squad leader was visibly relieved to find the defenses in SysTech hands - they had lost their C2 telepath to enemy fire, he explained, and had been without communications since.

Commander Harsing, Kerelle suspected, was just as relieved to see *them*. The commander had quickly tasked troops with fortifying the area, and when she dispatched a force to retrieve the scientists and their protectors from Zharala Prime, both the base and the retrieval team held significant enough numbers to forestall attack.

The SysTech force intended to stay put; with Demela Base in ashes, the cannons might as well be the locus of their defensive strength. It was a stopgap measure, and they all knew it. Zharal

V was not a large moon, and the defense cannons gave them control of the airspace - there would be no more ConEn bombing runs. On the orbitals scanners, however, it was a more sobering story. The ConEn fleet sat waiting, completely blockading the moon.

For the foreseeable future, nobody was going in or out.

FOURTEEN

BOLENDY SHIFTED NERVOUSLY in his seat. The conference chair had regained some equilibrium now that the group was safely ensconced in the new SysTech base, but a private interview with Kerelle was still a bit much for his nerves. She tried to project reassurance.

"I appreciate any help you can give me, Dr. Bolendy. If the missing people are still out there, they probably need aid, and I'll be able to find them more quickly if I know more about who I'm looking for." He looked a bit skeptical at that, and Kerelle had to privately agree. It wasn't great odds that the scientists stranded outside during the bombing run would be found safe and sound. But her mission was to bring back as many of the conference attendees as possible - and when she heard that Nalea was among those missing, she couldn't just give up. She owed it to Galhen to either find Nalea alive, or find definitive evidence she'd perished.

"I, ah, hope I don't disappoint you, agent," he replied, fiddling with the edge of his jacket. "The people we're missing are all preeminent in their fields, and I'm very familiar with their body of work, but we're not well acquainted personally."

"Anything you can give me will help," she told him, hoping she wasn't being overly optimistic. Bolendy settled in with a shade of resignation.

"Well, Dr. Cherden Meria Ellnor is the assistant department chair at Valla University, and he's most well known for his study on the cell regeneration effects of...."

It was a long afternoon. Kerelle took detailed notes on everything Bolendy could share; he was right, there wasn't much here besides their professional achievements, but hopefully it would be enough to point her in the right direction. They were nearing the end of the list when she straightened up.

"Dr. Nalea Tarau Ambrel, recently made division head at Olstenfel. Quite an accomplishment at her age, she's been a rising star for the past few years. Dr. Ambrel is a specialist in human-machine interfacing - ah, cybernetics," he clarified, seeing Kerelle's blank look. "She has contributed substantially to advances in integrating machine signals with the body, allowing for more responsive prosthetics."

Kerelle kept a straight face, but inside her excitement grew. A cybernetic specialist, it was almost too much to be true. Nalea might have some idea on how to get this damn collar off, or at least where to start. Of course Kerelle would have to *find* her first, and convince her to help. Thinking objectively, she realized with a note of chagrin, she had no idea what Nalea was like, or if introducing herself as Galhen's lover would get her anywhere.

Well, it was all a moot point if she was dead. Time to try and find out.

Their interview concluded, Kerelle headed back to the room she'd been using for quarters. It was small and cramped, but a little discomfort was worth it for the quiet and a door that locked. This was going to be hard enough *without* interruptions. There were C3 pure telepaths who specialized in locating specific minds from far away in a crowd, but to Kerelle it had always felt like searching for a diamond in a rocky beach.

She was tempted to go straight for Nalea, but she forced herself to be methodical and go down the list. First up was this Dr. Ellnor, from Valla University. She made herself as comfortable as she could and tried to clear her mind of everything but the goal. When she reached steady, measured breaths, she carefully opened her senses and reached out to the world beyond. Stray thoughts and feelings from around the base crowded her mind, but she determinedly pushed them down and stretched further beyond into the city.

She'd expected it would be bad, and she was correct. Outside their little makeshift fortress the city was a psychic minefield of fear and pain and grief. Teeth clenched, she kept herself steady and focused on thoughts of Dr. Ellnor. None of the impressions she was picking up felt right.

She ended up circling the city without any luck. Kerelle hoped it was an oversight on her part rather than an indication of Dr. Ellnor's fate, but she finally had to give up and move down the list to Dr. Undra. This one was more promising - she was able to pick up faint flashes of a mind that might be Undra's. It wasn't a firm read, but she sincerely doubted anyone else in the city would be thinking about mollusk adaptability at a time like this. Kerelle noted the direction she'd sensed and moved on.

Things went better after that. She was able to find leads for several more scientists, all in the same vicinity - including one that she thought might be Nalea. Relief flooded her; she might get her audience with Galhen's sister after all.

Assuming, of course, they got the missing scientists before anyone else did. Kerelle shared her findings with Commander Harsing, and in short order the commander had organized an extraction team to bring their wayward charges to safety. Kerelle would accompany them, both for added protection and to actually locate the scientists once they were close. She'd been able to sketch out a general area they were likely to be in, but between the distance and her lack of familiarity with the targets she couldn't pin down much more than that.

The team set out, aiming for a low profile despite the recent calm. Things had been quiet with ConEn since the battle of the defenses, and they assumed their opponents were holed up somewhere as well. The blockade was now a siege for both sides - SysTech couldn't leave as long as ConEn controlled orbital space, and ConEn couldn't land any more troops or supplies as long as SysTech controlled the planetary defenses. Harsing assumed that ConEn would mount a major offensive against the cannons at some point and was preparing accordingly, but for now both sides were dug in and conserving strength. Until the stalemate was broken, nobody was getting a resupply.

All this gave them a strong incentive to avoid open conflict with ConEn. Kerelle kept her senses wide open for any hint of the enemy as they cautiously ventured through the shattered street. As it turned out, luck was with them, and with Kerelle's early warning they were able to easily avoid the only ConEn group in the vicinity.

When they reached the area she'd designated on the map, it was time to get to work again. To Kerelle's relief, it was much easier this time - the minds she'd caught glimpses of before were now steady presences on the psychic landscape, like beacons they could follow to their destination. A bit more triangulation, a bit of searching, and they found a cluster of conference refugees huddled in the basement of a bombed-out shop.

The scientists were as wary of a heavily armed SysTech squad as Bolendy had been back at Zharala Prime. Unlike Bolendy, however, these were also cold and hungry and scared. It didn't take much talking to convince them they were being rescued. Another problem, however, immediately presented itself. They were still missing five people.

"Ellnor and Raltai are dead," Dr. Undra told her bluntly. The other woman's diminutive height belied her commanding presence; she seemed to have been the one to take charge of the wayward group and hustle it to shelter once disaster struck.

"Shrapnel in the bombing run. The rest of us have been lying low here and waiting for things to improve. Ambrel, Eskan, and Mauvel went out yesterday to search for supplies and never came back." She sighed wearily. "Maybe they're roasting marsh-mallows somewhere, but it seems most likely that they either got picked up by ConEn, or they're dead too. Either way, the rest of us weren't going to go out after them."

Kerelle thanked her for the information, though inside she wanted to scream. All this way and she still couldn't find Nalea. Maybe this hadn't been such a great plan after all. Part of her realized she was being irrational about all this - even if she found Nalea alive and unharmed, she had no idea if she would actually agree to help. Still, her earlier sentiment stood. Even if Nalea couldn't - or wouldn't - help her, Kerelle owed it to Galhen to see his sister to safety.

Now if only his sister didn't seem so determined to *run* from safety at every turn.

After a quick discussion with the head of the squad, it was determined that the soldiers would escort the scientists back to base while Kerelle stayed behind to scout for the remaining scientists. There was some risk to going alone, but the squad leader's arguments died when Kerelle flatly reminded him that she was the most dangerous thing out here.

She reached out her mind and tried again.

———

KERELLE CREPT FORWARD, keeping the ConEn squad firmly in her sights. They hadn't noticed her, and she was doing her utmost to keep it that way. *Nothing to look at here,* she projected gently. *Nothing to see. No reason to stop.*

She'd finally gotten a probable bead on Nalea, and she'd

followed it with increasing trepidation as she drew closer and closer to ConEn territory. The number and proximity of ConEn personnel had increased along the way, and now she was practically on their doorstep. She kept her mental shields dialed up tightly, to disguise her presence from any telepaths that might be keeping "watch." No one knew if there were more ConEn PsiCorp on Zharal V besides the ones she'd killed, but they had to assume that there were.

It was getting harder to ignore that she was taking a significant risk. Despite her words to the squad leader, she was hardly invincible, particularly against large groups of enemies that could overwhelm her shields. The responsible thing to do at this point would be to report back to base about what was going on - or at least check in with Parhet about the ConEn troop movements she was observing.

Kerelle was not feeling especially responsible. For the moment, she had a legitimate reason to be off the grid, and she intended to make the most of it.

She gauged the distance between the ConEn group and the next bit of cover. She'd been hoping they would continue on their way soon, but they'd been milling about for some time now and showed no sign of picking up again. She was going to have to sneak past them. Thank the stars that if ConEn *did* have any PsiCorp, they weren't with this group.

She intensified her projected telepathic encouragement. *Nothing in this direction is worth noting. Continue what you are doing, you see nothing, you have no reason to look here.* Cautiously, she slipped out of her hiding spot and crept toward the nearest cover. The trick would likely work, as long as they didn't have any reason to reconsider their impulse to ignore this area - like, say, a noise from a misplaced footstep. She scarcely breathed as she carefully put her feet down on solid asphalt, avoiding disturbing anything that might draw their attention. Just a bit further.

One of the ConEn soldiers idly shifted, his face turning in her direction. Kerelle froze and pushed as hard as she dared. *You see nothing, you see nothing, you see* nothing. But no, he *would* see her, and the shadows she was crouched in wouldn't be enough to convince him otherwise...

Inspiration struck, and she sent a telepathic shove against some rubble further down the street. She changed telepathic urgings immediately. *Suspicious! Investigate!*

Having them all on high alert would cause a *different* problem, of course, but she hoped to be long gone by the time they came back.

An instant of holding her breath to see if they would take the bait - and a soft exhale again as they did. The group ran down the street, guns ready to meet the suspicious threat. She practically ran the rest of the way to the sheltering walls of a half-collapsed building.

Satisfied no pursuit was imminent, she took a moment to collect her breath and examine her surroundings. It looked like she was in the remains of an office building, in what had probably been a conference room. Her senses told her Nalea was very close now, and she carefully searched the ruin for any signs the scientist had been here. The investigation turned up nothing, until she finally spotted the stairs down, half-hidden by a collapsed wall. Cautiously, Kerelle descended into the dark.

The stairs led into some sort of abandoned lab complex that would not be at all out of place in a horror movie. Kerelle firmly quashed her instinctive shivers and flicked on her portable light. If anything came shambling out of the shadows down here, she wouldn't be the one being torn apart.

Besides, Nalea was definitely down here - the signature she'd been following had grown steadily stronger as she came down the stairs, and now it was practically radiating. As Kerelle proceeded carefully into the lab, she swept out with her senses - and there she was, hidden behind a door a short ways away.

Nalea had heard her approach and ducked behind the broken door to hide. Kerelle sensed her fear and determination - and the small sidearm she was clutching like her life depended on it.

"Dr. Ambrel?" Kerelle called out softly. "Dr. Ambrel, this is Agent Evandra with SysTech. I'm here bring you to safety. Can you come out?"

There was no response, but Kerelle clearly picked up on her thoughts, this time colored with skepticism and indecision. Was it a good idea to comply? Was Kerelle really here to help her? What the hell was Nalea going to do if she wasn't? She didn't even know how to *fire* the gun. Maybe if she stayed quiet, Kerelle would go away.

Time to move this along. "Dr. Ambrel, I'm going to come in now. Please put down the firearm."

She caught a wave of resignation - Nalea knew she was hidden from view, which meant Kerelle was psionic, which meant resistance was futile - before she determinedly pulled back and shielded to keep from reading any more of Nalea's thoughts. She stepped into the room, and came face to face with a slightly older, female version of Galhen.

She was almost bodily shocked by how much they looked alike. The news photo didn't convey the half of it - the same expression, the same tilt of the head, the same golden hair and striking green eyes. *Focus*, Kerelle told herself forcefully. Nalea was *not* Galhen, and those beloved eyes were regarding her with unfamiliar mistrust.

First things first. "Dr. Ambrel, it's a relief to see you. My name is Kerelle Evandra, Class 3 telepath, Class 3 telekinetic with the SysTech PsiCorp. Dr. Bolendy sent me to find you and the others missing from the conference."

"I don't know who's left besides me. Eskan and Mauvel got picked up by ConEn, and I haven't seen anyone else since." Nalea's voice was low and angry, and Kerelle was briefly taken aback by her flat Istel inflection. Nalea looked so much like

Galhen, subconsciously Kerelle expected her to *sound* like him - but of course, Galhen's crisp Tallimau accent would have been acquired in the PsiCorp.

She recovered from her surprise at how Nalea spoke, and the implications sunk in of what Nalea had actually *said*. Oh dear. "We located a group with Dr. Undra, and they've been taken to safety. But you say the other two are in ConEn custody?" She tried to think of how to diplomatically ask if they'd been kidnapped.

Nalea saved her the trouble. "We spotted a ConEn patrol on our way in, and they figured any port in a storm. I decided to take my chances and took off before they flagged them down." She raised her eyebrows at Kerelle. "I've done enough work with multigalactics to know to read the fine print on any acts of altruism."

Sensible of her. Now Kerelle just needed to get that guard down a bit.

"No fine print this time," she answered truthfully. "As the contracted security provider for the conference, SysTech's retainer includes your personal safety - which is why I'm here to escort you back to a secured area. Are you hurt at all, Dr. Ambrel?"

"Just a few bruises." Nalea crossed her arms irritably. "Not bad considering we've spent the last two days dodging bombs, shrapnel and stars know what else. Do I get to deduct from your *retainer* for that?"

If the university sued for it, quite possibly. This was shaping up to be an expensive, embarrassing debacle for SysTech, but Kerelle couldn't muster up much sympathy for her employer's bruised image - or for whoever internally would take the fall. *Someone's* career would likely end over this, but it wouldn't be anyone in the PsiCorp, and as far as she was concerned the people that allowed this whole terrible, *unnecessary* shitshow to unfold deserved what was coming to them.

Focus. Now that she'd found Nalea alive and unhurt, she needed to talk to her, and that wasn't going to happen back at the base. Besides, it was getting dark, and the area was crawling with ConEn. The decision she was about to make was only partially self-serving.

Nalea did not look pleased when Kerelle explained that they would spend the night in the ruins and depart in the morning, after the ConEn presence had hopefully moved on. But she didn't protest either, and in short order they established a makeshift camp. Kerelle discreetly moved a bit of rubble to better disguise the stairs down to their creepy basement, and watched Nalea tear ravenously into the ration bars she'd brought in her pack.

Satisfied that her charge was fed and as comfortable as she was going to get, Kerelle took a deep breath and dove in.

FIFTEEN

"DR. AMBREL, I'd hoped we could meet under better circumstances, but this will have to do. I have a private matter I need to discuss with you, and I don't know when I'll get another chance."

Nalea looked up from her ration bar, regarding Kerelle warily. The back of Kerelle's mind was screaming at her - what was she *doing*, this was madness, she didn't know this woman at all. The plan that seemed perfectly reasonable in her head suddenly looked startlingly reckless as she confronted it in reality. Nalea could turn around and report her to SysTech, and *oh stars* don't think about what they would do to her.

She faltered a moment before the enormity of it, then steeled herself to continue. *Take a risk, or stay "safe" and give up.*

"I know we've only just met, but I...I need your help." The scientist's eyebrows rose, but she stayed silent as Kerelle continued. "It's about your brother, actually. Galhen."

At the mention of her brother, Nalea's expression went shuttered, though a slight widening of her eyes betrayed her shock. Still she said nothing, and after a moment's awkward silence Kerelle stumbled on.

"Galhen and I are...." What, exactly? *Lovers* sounded so shallow, *partners* so anodyne. *Each others' missing halves,* so melodramatic.

"Very close," she finally finished, not sure that was much better. "Earlier this year, his contract was sold to some senator from the Morafer system. The last time I saw him was months ago."

She paused again, trying to think of the right words, and Nalea spoke for the first time.

"I don't see what that has to do with me." Her eyes avoided Kerelle's.

"I think he needs help," Kerelle explained in a rush. So much for the right words - she needed to get to the point before she lost Nalea entirely.

"I saw the records - the senator has been using his collar to hurt him. And SysTech won't do anything, they got their money and now they don't care. No one cares, except me, and there's nothing I can do to help him. Not as long as I'm wearing this." She gestured at the collar in disgust. "And not as long as he's wearing *his.*"

She leaned in towards Nalea, who still determinedly avoided her gaze. "When I learned you were a cybernetics expert, I thought you might be able to help get the collars off. I know what I'm asking, but - "

"No," Nalea cut her off. "I don't think you do." Her voice held unexpected heat. "That you're even *asking* me this is putting my entire life at risk."

Nalea gestured angrily, and Kerelle drew back in spite of herself at the unexpected vehemence. "You can't just...just walk in here out of nowhere and ask me to risk destroying my career and *getting shot by SysTech* like you're asking to crash on my couch. You could get an inquiry opened on me just by *talking* about this!"

"I'm sorry," Kerelle replied, nonplussed. "I wouldn't...we're alone here, and this stays between us."

Nalea's face flushed, but she still wouldn't look at Kerelle. "I'm sorry things are...going rough for you. But I'm not risking my life for a couple of strangers."

Kerelle couldn't blame her for that, not really, even as a bleak, despairing weariness began to settle over her bones. If there was one thing Kerelle understood, it was protecting herself. And yet...

"I know *I'm* a stranger," she answered quietly. "And I understand why you wouldn't do it for me. But it's your brother who needs help. Would you consider it for *him?*"

"I don't know him either," Nalea growled, but there was a different undercurrent now to her voice, and to her sudden rush of projected feeling. The anger was still there - anger, covering for fear. But underneath those sharp feelings rippled something else, like a deep pool disturbed by a pebble.

Sadness, Kerelle thought it was; sadness and guilt.

"I haven't seen Galhen since he was 8 and I was 13. I don't even remember what he looks like. And," her brow pinched, and though her voice was harsh the sadness in her aura intensified. "After all this time I'm sure he doesn't remember *me.*"

Kerelle blinked. "But of course he does. I knew who you were because Galhen saw your promotion in the news, and he was so happy for you. He said you always loved learning as a child, and he was proud you'd done so well for yourself."

Nalea didn't answer; Kerelle hoped that meant she was listening. She kept going.

"Growing up in the PsiCorp we weren't supposed to talk about our families. SysTech tried to keep us busy, and I think they hoped we would just forget who we'd been before the program." Not that Kerelle had any memories to lose anyway, but this wasn't about her. "But when we were away from our teachers, Galhen used to tell me stories about growing up in Istel City, with you and your brother and your parents. I think talking about it helped him remember, and he didn't *want* to forget you."

"Couldn't blame him if he did," Nalea muttered. She leaned her head back against the well, still avoiding eye contact. Louder, she added, "I can't imagine what he could have had to say about me."

Kerelle thought back. "That you were the more fun of his siblings, if I recall. You were always the one who would play games and take him to the park to race boats in the creek, because your other brother was older and didn't want to be bothered."

She snorted softly. "Yes, that sounds like Balheren."

It went quiet then, and Kerelle cast about for something else to say. Nalea's body language remained defensive, hunched against the other wall with her knees drawn tightly against her chest, but it felt as though they'd been approaching a fragile rapport. There had to be *something* she could do to continue it.

The scientist surprised her, however, by speaking first.

"So...what's he like, now?" She darted a quick glance over at Kerelle. "Galhen."

Kerelle told her. She started with simple generalities, his warmth and humor and compassion, but almost before she'd realized it everything from the last few months came spilling out. Galhen treating civilians on Elekar, exhausting himself the first night to save wounded soldiers from permanent disability, offering comfort to her when he was worn out and stressed and sick with horror himself.

"Please, Dr. Ambrel," she finished softly. "Galhen is your brother, and he still loves you. But more than that he's a good man, and he deserves better than this." She lifted her eyes to finally meet Nalea's, and was surprised to see they glinted with unshed tears. "I know that what I'm asking is dangerous, and you don't owe us anything. But *please*. No one else can help."

Nalea was silent, for long enough that Kerelle thought that that was her answer. A dull ache of defeat started spreading through her chest, when the other woman raised her voice into the darkness.

"I'll think about it."

THE NEXT MORNING found them cold and sore, but better rested than Kerelle would have expected for a night spent in a creepy ruin. They said nothing of what had been passed between them the night before, and Nalea was brooding and withdrawn. A weary disappointment settled in Kerelle's gut as she broke down their little camp and doled out the last of the ration bars.

Abruptly, Nalea set down her ration bar and broke the silence.

"I don't promise anything. This whole idea is completely insane and if we get caught even *thinking* about it we'll both be screwed." She sighed deeply then and finally looked up at Kerelle. "But if we can find a sample collar to do some tests with, I'll look into it."

Kerelle's giddy surprise almost took her breath away - then she deflated just as quickly.

"Trying to steal a collar won't be easy. It might take me some time to figure it out."

Nalea didn't quite roll her eyes. "Actually I was hoping to find one down here in the labs." She arched an eyebrow at Kerelle's confused look. "Didn't you know? These are Stellar-Eye's old cybernetics research labs."

Kerelle nearly sat down. "Are you serious? Here? What are the odds?"

This time Nalea almost smirked. "Why do you think I was out here in the first place? Seemed like a good opportunity to see if they left anything interesting behind."

If she'd been surprised before, now Kerelle was utterly astounded. She managed a shaky laugh. "Why Dr. Ambrel, what would Dr. Bolendy say if he knew you were here to loot in the name of science?"

"He'd be mad he didn't think of it first. Here, take the light and let's get this over with. I imagine we don't have infinite time before somebody comes looking for us. Oh, and call me Nalea," she added dryly over her shoulder. "I think plotting felonies together puts us on first-name basis."

The search was on.

From Kerelle's perspective, it did not seem promising. From the scattered detritus to the thick layer of dust that coated it, the lab had obviously been abandoned for some time. What equipment remained didn't look like it had been top of the line.

"Do you really think we're going to find anything useful here? I would think that StellarEye would have taken anything of value with them when they left."

"Eh, yes and no." Nalea's voice was slightly muffled by the desk she was rooting around beneath. "From what I understand they shut down pretty quickly at the end. It's possible the staff would have been locked out when the liquidation hit. Or," she added pointedly, "they might have cut and run to avoid getting kidnapped when the SysTech and ConEn teams landed."

It was not her first comment to that effect, and Kerelle tamped down her irritation. If there was anything she could do about SysTech's actions, she wouldn't be here asking for Nalea's help, would she?

But she *was* asking for Nalea's help, so she only nodded and stayed silent. Initially she'd tried to help with searching, but she had no real idea what they were looking for. After Nalea's annoyed sigh at her third question, Kerelle reluctantly accepted that her utility was mainly in holding the light. Judging by Nalea's gleeful squeal at finding a datastick that had fallen between two drawers, she was at least finding what *she* had come here for. Kerelle's hope of finding anything relevant to her own situation was beginning to fade, when the last labspace turned up the jackpot.

Kerelle's breathing sped up as she held the light steady, and realized what she was looking at. Sitting on the lab counter was a fully intact collar, and beside it another that looked partially disassembled.

"Nalea, is this what we need? Right here?"

The scientist picked up the collar and examined it dispassionately. "Sure seems to be. Might not be the same model as yours but the functional components should be the same. And look, they even went to the trouble of taking it apart so I don't have to." She grabbed both collars and fussed with getting them into her pack, grumbling that she hadn't planned to pick up anything so bulky. There was a certain light in the scientist's eyes, however - for all her protests, she was intrigued by the challenge. Another point of resemblance to her brother.

"Let's look around. If these were here, there might be more."

They didn't find any additional collars, but judging by the equipment left behind, the study and improvement of collars seemed to have been the little lab's focus. The previous occupants hadn't left tablets or note-taking devices behind, unfortunately - but when Kerelle poked the light into a corner, it revealed an old fixed-computing station, tucked against the wall.

It took up most of the desk it was sitting on. Judging by the style, Kerelle thought it might be almost as old as they were. Whatever limited funding StellerEye might have been able to provide near the end of its life, this lab clearly had not been first in line. A small note was affixed to the side, facing the wall - *StellarEye123*.

Kerelle stared at it. "That can't be the password."

"Sure it can. Easy to remember, easy to spell, not that you need to do either when it's posted on the machine. Who's going to break in down here and see it? Besides us, apparently." Nalea sounded amused at that last part.

"But surely...I mean...SysTech has all kinds of policies around this kind of thing, I would have thought StellarEye would too."

"And I'm sure each and *every one* of those policies is followed to the *letter* at SysTech." Nalea didn't bother to disguise her mocking tone. She gave Kerelle a sidelong glance. "I'm not sure if I should be relieved or scared that the mighty PsiCorp are as naive as my first-year interns. Now scoot, and let me get in there."

Nalea slid into the old desk chair, heedless of the small dust cloud that erupted around her. "I imagine this thing's internal backup power is way tapped out." She pressed the power-on button to no effect and nodded. "Can you shine the light right over here?"

Nalea rummaged in her pack and came up with a tiny screwdriver and a small metallic brick - a battery like the one the fixed workstation likely used for failover in the event of power loss. In this case the failover had long since failed as well; they were intended more to keep a workstation functional long enough to save data than as a real alternative power source. The station had probably sputtered out within an hour or two.

Not that that seemed to present much problem to Nalea. She deftly unscrewed the face of the workstation and rearranged a few wires to introduce her little power brick to the array, and was rewarded by the soft tone of the station booting up. The screen flared to life, bathing the dark room in sudden light.

"Do you *usually* carry tools and backup power sources?" Kerelle asked curiously. Being an academic was starting to look more rough-and-tumble than she'd imagined.

"I came prepared for this." Nalea waved a hand vaguely as she entered the password into the OS prompt. "I figured if anything *was* still down here, it would probably need some coaxing to be accessible. Aha!" She grinned at Kerelle, vivid eyes sparkling, and for a moment she looked so much like Galhen that Kerelle's chest ached. "We're in. Let's see what they left us."

Nalea popped open the file index and scrolled down. "My, there's more here than I thought there would be. More than we've got time for, probably." She produced another data transfer stick and thrust it into the workstation's port. "I'll just grab the whole thing and look through it later."

They took another quick turn around the room as the transfer progress bar inched painfully forward, but even with the additional light from the workstation's screen, there wasn't anything left of interest. They ended up leaning against the counters to wait in awkward silence.

Nalea abruptly spoke. "So you and my brother."

"Yes," Kerelle answered. She wasn't quite sure what Nalea was asking, but she looked like she expected more of a response. "We've been together for over ten years now." She blinked as she added it up in her head. "Close to fifteen, actually. Almost half our lives."

Nalea gave her a sideways glance. "I didn't think PsiCorp were really into long-term relationships. Long-term anything."

"We're not supposed to be," she admitted. "Galhen and I have had to be discreet. It's not technically breaking any rules, but it's definitely discouraged."

"How does *that* work?"

"Well…" Kerelle raised her eyes to the dark ceiling, trying to think of how to explain. She decided to back up a bit. "I know the PsiCorp has a certain reputation."

"Self-centered materialists with no morals," Nalea supplied helpfully.

"Yes," Kerelle agreed, trying to keep the flash of annoyance out of her voice. She might not appreciate the assessment, but Nalea wasn't wrong. "The thing is that we *are* raised with a strong sense of right and wrong - it's just that the company's version of that is that 'right' is putting our work before anything and everything else. The 'right thing to do' is to do as you're told with no hesitation, no matter how much you don't want to."

She paused for a moment. This was moving a bit closer to subjects Kerelle didn't feel comfortable discussing. The village on Elekar flashed again in her mind, and she resolutely pushed it away. Thinking about that now wouldn't help anything.

"What I'm getting at is that, yes, that reputation is somewhat earned. Growing up in the PsiCorp, we're encouraged to chase our own pleasure - but only as long as it doesn't interfere with our work and our dedication to serving the company. SysTech doesn't care if you're high on ambrosia every night, so long as you can do what's asked of you in the morning. We can sleep with anyone and everyone we want, so long as you wave goodbye with no complications when it's time for your next mission. Casual sex is one thing, but they don't like us getting *attached*. I think the company is afraid that being in love might lead to..."

"This?" Nalea answered sardonically, gesturing to encompass themselves, the lab, the slowly plodding workstation.

Kerelle sighed and slumped back against the wall. "Yes. This exactly."

It was quiet again for a minute. It was Nalea who spoke first again.

"It seems like you have it pretty good in the PsiCorp though. Is he *really* worth all this?"

"Yes," she answered immediately. It was the truth. But it wasn't the whole truth...and given what Nalea was risking for her, she probably deserved that whole truth, whether Kerelle was comfortable discussing it or not.

"Yes," she repeated, sighing. "He is. Galhen is a better person than I could ever be, and a better partner than I could ever deserve. I would trade every comfort in the galaxy to have him safe in my arms. But the truth is that leaving the PsiCorp won't be much of a sacrifice."

She paused for a moment, willing herself to continue. She'd never been comfortable speaking plainly about her feelings; even Galhen sometimes had to suss it out of her. *Steady on, Kerelle. You owe her this.*

"I've always been a good girl and done what was asked of me, and what's asked of me is destruction. At first it was just because it was my duty, because I believed what I was taught that it was the right thing to do, even when it felt wrong. I felt guilty that it bothered me, because the company gave us so much, and I thought there must have been something wrong with *me*, that I was ungrateful enough to question. But fine wine and luxury handbags don't wash off blood."

She toyed with her sleeve, avoiding Nalea's eyes. "Later...later I didn't feel so much like I owed them anything, but what else could I do? The collar meant they could kill me for disobeying them, or worse. Galhen and I didn't flaunt our relationship, but management must have known something." *Everyone else apparently did.* "What if they hurt him to get to me? As long as we did what we were told and didn't argue, we believed we'd be safe. And look how *that* turned out."

"So no," she finished heavily. "I'm not giving up the good life to chase down my lover. I'm not torching a high-powered career. The PsiCorp has *always* been a cage, even if it took me a long time to realize it. And it's a cage I'm going to break us both out of, even if it kills me."

It was silent for a beat before Nalea finally replied. "Yes... well...let's hope it doesn't."

They were both relieved when the transfer finally completed with a plaintive beep, as if the workstation knew its brief resurrection was coming to an end. Nalea replaced the now-full datastick to a discreet pocket and powered the workstation down, retrieving her battery and connectors as well.

"I think that's the best we're going to do down here," she declared. "We might as well head back to your base." She grimaced slightly. "Not exactly sure how well it's going to go trying to study these under SysTech's nose, but I'm guessing they'll have bigger concerns than whatever a bunch of academics are doing."

"They will," Kerelle assured her. *Honestly,* she thought, *Harsing will just be glad she's being quiet and staying out of the way.* Aloud she added, "Besides, the SysTech personnel are almost all military. They won't know what you're looking at. Your fellow scientists are probably the bigger threat of discovery."

Nalea rolled her eyes. "Do you think I got to be a department head because I was just *that good* at research? I know how to deal with my esteemed colleagues."

Kerelle tried to keep herself from getting excited as they packed up and cautiously ventured out of their erstwhile shelter. There were still many hurdles to clear and many, many things that could go wrong. But as the warm sun hit her face and she led Nalea down the now-clear streets, she couldn't help the little sparks of hope that danced in her mind. They could find a way.

SIXTEEN

KERELLE SHIELDED her eyes against the late-afternoon sun, keeping her senses extended as the rest of her patrol hustled their finds into the mechanized cart. She could sense a ConEn group, but only dimly. They were still quite a ways off, and with luck they would stay that way.

Scavenging for supplies had become significantly more hazardous as the days dragged into weeks. Initially they'd been able to find what they needed near their adopted base at the planetary defenses, but those easy pickings were now exhausted. Lately they'd been forced to range further afield, and closer to ConEn territory. There was a reason Kerelle now accompanied scavenging parties.

The scavenging trips represented the only break in the stifling monotony of the base, which had grown nearly unbearable in the endless high-alert holding pattern. It still felt wrong to admit that she looked forward to them.

"That's all of it, ma'am," one of them called. "Think we're ready to head back?" Kerelle glanced back at the cart, now full to the top. They'd had a good find in this as-yet-unlooted warehouse.

She nodded her agreement. "Let's go, sergeant. I want to get back before we lose the light."

She kept a mental watch on the ConEn group as they retraced their way to the base. They were slightly closer now, but still out of danger range - either they didn't know the SysTech group was there, or they had a telepath of their own guiding them away in turn. ConEn brass likely didn't want to waste resources on skirmishing any more than SysTech did.

The ConEn group stayed back, but she picked up another presence - or rather, a group of presences. Curious, she leaned in further. *Oh.*

It was a group of civilians, huddled in one of the half-collapsed buildings and nervously waiting for their group to pass. Kerelle realized with a pang of guilt that they'd probably been hoping to get some of that same food. Most of Zharal's citizens had fled to parts of the city further from the multigalactics' main presence. If these were here, they were probably fairly desperate.

Kerelle cast a surreptitious glance back at the cart. The patrol was scanning the horizons for trouble, trusting the mechanized cart to trundle on without direct supervision. Which meant nobody was closely watching its contents.

She delicately wrapped her telekinetics around a small stack of nutrition bars near the bottom, careful not to overturn the rest of the stack. Feeling mildly guilty for using her abilities on her own people, she projected inattention on her squad, then jostled the cart as though it had run over a rough patch of ground.

She had her little stack of bars safely hidden by the side of the road before the patrol finished investigating the cart's problem. Kerelle raised her eyes to the building that sheltered the civilians, and ever so slightly inclined her head towards the secret cache. Hopefully someone was watching and would understand.

They were soon on their way again, but the incident continued to bother her. As distasteful and uncompelling as she'd found Helneres's views about the Elekari - that they'd brought their suffering on themselves by challenging SysTech - one could argue they'd held a kernel of truth. Here, there wasn't even that thin excuse. These people had done *nothing* to invite this catastrophe, nothing but live near a prize two dueling multigalactics had wanted. Whoever at SysTech ultimately took the blame for the Zharal incident would lose their position and possibly a portion of their wealth, but it was the civilians here who paid the true price for SysTech's greed and stupidity.

And once again, here she was in the middle of it. She'd felt good for a moment offering the civilians food, but the guilt rushed in again just as quickly. So she helped a few people not go to sleep hungry. How many nutrition bars balanced out a pile of dead Elekari?

One way or another, this conflict needed to wrap up. It was like Galhen had noted on Elekar - the only way to improve things for civilians was for the multigalactic forces to *leave*.

––––––––

IF KERELLE and the soldiers were getting restless at the base, the scientists were practically climbing the walls. They'd been confined to a small part of the base for their own safety, and the initial terror that had kept them compliant faded as time ground on with no resolution in sight. This ended up working in Kerelle and Nalea's favor - fed up with constant harping, Harsing permitted the scientists to set up research stations to keep them occupied. Nobody looked twice at Nalea studying her purloined files.

Kerelle understood these things took time and tried to keep her patience under control. All the same, when a message popped up from Nalea, it was a struggle to keep her excitement in check.

It said nothing, of course - just an impersonal request to consult on a matter of scientific research. But Kerelle knew it had to be about the collars. With an effort, she schooled her face into casual indifference and went to find out what her destiny held.

"Dr. Ambrel? You asked to speak with me?" She tried to sound slightly bored.

"I did, but..." Nalea looked around with her eyes narrowed. "Someplace more private. My research is pre-patent and I would prefer discretion." She shot a dark glance at a small cluster of scientists who were watching their interaction with interest.

Kerelle affected an eyeroll. "Of course, Doctor." She made a show of her patient indulgence as she escorted her to a private room.

Safely behind the closed door, Nalea's agitation only increased.

"I still can't believe I'm doing this. I can't believe I *did* this. But I think I found something."

She pulled up a carefully-annotated document on her tablet. "There was a treasure trove of information on that drive, including every major paper on collars and psionic physiology in the last 15 years."

Kerelle raised her eyebrows. "Are there a lot of those?"

"Stars, yes. Figuring out what makes psionics *psionic* is pretty much the ultimate dream in genetics research. I mean, clearly there's a physiological component, since psionics universally respond to dermal contact with hemindrium." Kerelle gave her a blank look. "The active component in your collar," she clarified with a tone of incredulity.

With a faintly disgusted noise, Nalea resumed her explanation. Her voice took on the tone and cadence of a lecture. "Besides hemindrium there are of course other shared physical traits, most obviously that psionics appear to be universally sterile. Even in a lab setting, no one has ever been able to coax viable offspring from psionic genetic material." She looked pointedly up at Kerelle. "You knew *that* at least, I hope?"

Kerelle felt her cheeks warm as she nodded. Nalea continued. "Just as obviously, however, it's not genetic. Despite exhaustive research there's been no evidence found that it runs in families as a recessive trait. Not that that stops the multi-galactics from wishful thinking, Balheren and I were both tested again after Galhen was taken, just in case they missed us the first time." She rolled her eyes. "For stars' sake, Balheren was *fifteen*. Manifesting psionic gifts at that age would be like getting a sudden growth spurt in your forties.

"But back to my point: no genetic link, nothing conclusive about environments, nothing conclusive about ancestry traits. There seems to just be a small random chance that two perfectly unremarkable human parents will produce a psionic child, and it drives researchers nuts. The multigalactics would *love* to grow their PsiCorp to order in a lab instead of having to prowl around looking for gifted kids. Anyone who cracks the psionic code is going to be very rich." She shrugged. "So far, though, just a lot of grant money down the drain. Seriously, you didn't know all this?"

"Pondering one's place in the universe wasn't exactly encouraged in the PsiCorp - and neither was pondering where you came from. And they certainly never taught us *anything* about the collars, except for the ways they could be used against us. They did cover the sterility thing in our health courses. Briefly."

Nalea pinched the bridge of her nose. "No wonder we never get researchers out of the PsiCorp. The important thing is, I think I found a way around the collar." She peered at Kerelle again. "Have you seriously been wearing that thing your whole life, and you have no idea how it works?"

"We knew they *did* work. The *how* never seemed all that important."

Nalea took a deep breath and let it back out.

"Okay, so way back, someone discovered that psionics shared weird sensitivity to hemindrium, though again, no one knows why. This was eventually refined to create the collars, which sync with the subject's nervous system and can use that connection to administer painful or fatal feedback."

"Yes, I'm quite familiar with that part."

"So the thing is, they weren't designed to come off. I'm assuming they told you not to mess with them when you were kids? That wasn't propaganda, it really will kill you if you try to brute-force it off. If there's a way to disengage one, it's locked up tight in a vault somewhere. The StellarEye scientists weren't interested in removal, and there are no records anywhere I could find about safe removal methods."

"I assume there's a 'but' in here somewhere?"

"But I may have come up with one," Nalea confirmed. "Or, well, *a* removal method. The safe part is pretty questionable."

She withdrew a vial from her coat. "So this substance here has proven effective in dampening human-machine connections in some of my other work. Granted that wasn't with hemindrium, but the principle should be the same.

"But it's unlikely to be enough to shut the collar down on its own," she continued, producing another vial. "Which is where this one comes in. This is a suppressant. The active ingredient is a chemical relative of hemindrium, and it will knock out your psionics until it wears off."

Kerelle drew back. "I didn't know that was possible."

Nalea glanced between her and the vial. "You're not making a strong argument for the PsiCorp educational system."

Kerelle stared at the vial in her hand, feeling vaguely unsettled. "I'm going to guess the omission was intentional." Apparently SysTech had more weapons against rogue psionics than just the ones they were told about. She wondered what other surprises there were.

"The plan is this: the collar is synced to your system. If your vitals go down, it has to work that much harder to stay synced. We prep you with the dampener and the suppressant, which will weaken the collar's efficacy. And then," she shifted both vials into one hand and produced another, "we hit you with a drug cocktail to stop your heart for a few seconds. The combined effect should be enough to knock the collar offline, giving me a seconds-long window to cut the connection."

Nalea replaced the vials to her pocket and glanced at Kerelle. "By the way, I mentioned this plan is completely insane and liable to get you killed, right? We're clear on that?"

Kerelle stared at the floor. It *did* sound completely insane, and it *did* sound likely to kill her, and she couldn't deny the cold fear that squirmed in her gut. What was she willing to do to see Galhen again? What was she willing to do to be free?

Anything, her heart whispered. She straightened up to meet Nalea's eyes.

"I'll do it."

SEVENTEEN

THEY HAD A PLAN. But a few days later, after she'd had some time to think it over, it was apparent they also had several new problems.

"When we accomplish this," Kerelle noted - *when, not if, never if* - "we're going to have to get off Zharal V in a hurry. We'll also need to discourage SysTech from looking for me."

"Definitely that last part," Nalea agreed. "And no arguments here on getting off the moon. Any ideas on *how*?"

"The discouragement part is easier. If we're going to stop my heart in surgery -" she managed to get the words out with nonchalance, as if this were perfectly reasonable occurrence and not absolutely terrifying - "we might as well go the whole way to fake my death.

"The collar links back to the SysTech main systems," she explained to Nalea's raised eyebrows. "They're not constantly sending data, that would be way too much, but they auto-generate reports if something significant happens." That was, after all, how she knew what had happened to Galhen. "My vitals flatlining would definitely count as a significant reporting event. If we can come up with something convincing, they might just write me off as KIA. It may not work forever, but should at least buy us some time."

"That's not a bad idea," Nalea replied. "The collar powers itself by absorbing energy from the subject, so once I separate it from you, I think it will just turn off. Which will support the idea that you're dead." She shrugged. "Seems like as good a plan as any. Now for that escape part."

Kerelle sighed. "That part is harder. It's not like we can just hop a commercial flight with ConEn still blockading the whole moon."

"Yeah, and considering you're going to be 'dead,' without any not-dead ID, that probably wouldn't be such a great idea anyway." True. Convincing an entire commercial shuttle flight to *just not look at her* for hours sounded like something even Galhen would have trouble with.

"At the same time, if we wait until the blockade is broken, our escape window narrows considerably. SysTech will consolidate its hold on the moon, I'll be recalled back to Tallimau for my next assignment, and there goes our chance of getting out quietly. What we really *need*," Kerelle mused, "is someone with their own ship, who can make it past a corporate military blockade - and is willing to try in the first place. Stars know where we're going to find *that*."

"Well," Nalea answered thoughtfully, "it sounds to me like what you just described is a *smuggler*, and Zharal V's as good a place as any to find one. You really think all those bioresearch materials were on the up-and-up?"

Kerelle had thought that actually, and Nalea's earlier comment about being naive as a first-year intern rose unbidden in her mind. Apparently being an academic *was* rather more exciting than it sounded.

"Granted I'm not sure how to actually find one," Nalea continued. She tapped a finger absentmindedly against her cheek. "I always bought from grey-market middlemen. Or of course, I *would* have," she added with a glint in her eye, "if I would have ever *dreamed* of doing such a thing. But assuming they're still here, probably the pilot bars by the spaceport are a good place to start?"

BY THE TIME Kerelle was able to slip away from the base, the sun had dropped below the battered skyline to give way to a murky twilight. The first few nights Zharal had been dark as the void, the only light gently wafting down from the distant stars. Near their makeshift base, in the erstwhile downtown where the bombs had hit the hardest, it still was - once you left the wan fluorescents of the fortified defense system, the neighborhoods were little more than rubble and ruin, darkened bones jutting out of Zharal's flesh.

The darkness was no longer all-encompassing, however. Faint lights glowed in the distance, more visible against the unremitting black of the immediate streets than they might otherwise be. From the looks of it, civilian authorities had managed to restore at least some power to the relatively unscathed parts of the city.

Good for them. As far as Kerelle knew, Zharal's mayor and city council had been entirely ignored by both the SysTech and ConEn forces. Doubtlessly when one or the other emerged victorious, they'd see about either installing their own civilian government or assuring the submission of the current one. For now, each was only focused on their own survival and victory, and it gave her some hope to see that *someone*, at least, was looking out for Zharal itself.

She headed towards those welcome lights. It was a long walk to the dock, and a relief to pass out of the downtown's lonely bones into the areas lit with some indication of human life. Kerelle had left her PsiCorp jacket behind for a hooded coat that offered some anonymity - and most importantly, obscured her collar. It was a rare opportunity to observe the world, unnoticed and unidentified as PsiCorp.

The city might be unrecognizable from when she had landed, but it was still there. As she drew closer to the docks the streets gradually came alive again with the glow of streetlights and occupied buildings, and people out and about. Shops had reopened, some outside under rough tarps, some in heavily-boarded storefronts. Kerelle could sense fear and uncertainty in the people all around her, but also a pragmatic determination to reclaim their lives and establish a new normal. They wouldn't, couldn't hide in their basements indefinitely.

The spaceport itself seemed to have been largely spared in the bombings - probably because ConEn had intended to use it soon after. For that reason, perhaps, it was one of the more lively spots she'd passed through. The bars that lined its neighboring street were not only open, but *full*. She chose one that looked appropriately downmarket and headed in.

The interior was dimmer than the twilit street, illuminated only by a cluster of sparse, flickering fixtures above the bar. Shadows pooled deep in the room's corners, lending an aura of obscurity to the patrons who occupied its small tables alone or in quiet groups. A sharp smell lingered in the air, of cheap cleaning spray and cheaper liquor.

It certainly *seemed* like the kind of place to find a smuggler.

Kerelle made her way to the small bar, more as a cover than anything. She tapped her telepathy to gently broadcast the suggestion that she was no one to take note of - just another stranded spacer, looking for a drink. Not that anyone was inclined to take note of her anyway, she quickly realized; from the projected feelings in the room, these people had their own problems.

On all sides, she read frustration, cynicism, and under it all the cold froth of fear. These people were trapped just like she was, without even what security SysTech's strength in numbers could provide. Bubbling fiercely was fear for both their livelihoods and their lives - and hatred for the multigalactics, whose callous bullshit had put all of them in this position.

Well, she could certainly relate to that feeling. All the same, she slouched lower into the shallow refuge of her coat's high collar, further concealing the alloy band at her throat. Civilian clothing or not, one good look at the collar and there would be no question that she was PsiCorp. In a room full of strangers angry at her bosses, recognizably PsiCorp was not something she wanted to be.

Gathering her best nerves, she approached the bartender with a smile.

"Whiskey on the rocks," she addressed him casually. He gave a grunt of acknowledgement and grabbed a bottle. Kerelle grimaced inwardly at the label; cheaper liquor indeed.

Outwardly, she smiled again and leaned in a bit closer. "How's business been?"

"Same as everywhere, I imagine," he answered neutrally, not looking at her as he measured the pour. "Lots of customers, limited supplies." He pushed the glass over to her, finally flicking his eyes over to hers. "Twenty credits."

Limited supplies indeed, if that was the going rate for 50 milliliters of Halgen's (bottom-of-the) Barrel-Aged.

She plunked down the money and a generous tip, and lowered her voice. "Any news on when you might get a resupply?"

He raised his eyebrows at her. "That's up to the corporate folks, isn't it. Sooner they decide who's killing who, the sooner the rest of us get to move on."

She glanced around and leaned back in. "That's a long time to wait. Surely there's some talent around here that could speed things up."

"I wouldn't know," he answered brusquely, and pointedly

moved away to stack glasses at the back of the bar. The thoughts dancing at the surface of his mind, however, said otherwise.

Sandrel. Sandrel Dani Marene could do it. He slipped the siege at Cahl Vorna, he's made dozens of high-risk smuggling runs without a scratch, he can do this. But this suspicious strange woman sure isn't going to hear it from me.

Kerelle tapped the bar to get his attention and lifted her drink. "Actually, can I get a second one of these?"

───────

SHE SCANNED the room for the person who matched the bartender's thoughts, condensation on the second glass already beginning to drip. Aha - the man sitting in the corner, his own drink mostly gone. Before she could think better of it, she headed over.

"Is this seat taken?" she asked warmly, gesturing to the seat opposite him. She set one of the drinks down on his side. "I come bearing gifts."

"In that case, the seat's all yours." He gestured for her to sit down with a broad smile that was more practiced charm than genuine warmth. She didn't need telepathy to know his guard was all the way up.

Kerelle took a long sip of her whiskey, using the space to take his measure. Sandrel Dani Marene was probably a few years older than her, but still short of forty. His appearance was pleasant, but not particularly memorable - light brown hair cut in a style that was current without being trendy, symmetrical features that were attractive without being striking. The same went for his clothing - nondescript, but all good quality and condition. That seemed promising.

He sipped the drink and watched her, expression set in a bland mask. He had to be curious what she wanted, but he wasn't going to give anything away by asking first.

That seemed promising, too.

Might as well get to it, then. She leaned forward.

"I hear you're the man to see about a ride out of here. And not from the bartender," she added hastily as his dark eyes cut behind her. "So don't blame him."

"I don't know who you heard it from, then," he answered nonchalantly, taking a sip of his whiskey. "Moon's blockaded. Nobody's giving rides anywhere."

Kerelle lowered her voice. "Word is that might not be a problem for you." She'd come prepared for this meeting, and eased a heavily jeweled ring off her finger. She slid it across the table to him. "Proof of intent."

Sandrel picked it up gave it a critical inspection, then looked back to her. "An awfully expensive ride." His eyebrows raised slightly, in the unspoken question of *why*.

A question she did not intend to answer. "That should work in your favor, then." She held his gaze. "I'll pay twice that to get off Zharal V in two days, along with a friend. Half now, half when we arrive at the nearest neutral port."

"A *very* expensive ride," he repeated, watching her. "Zharal V's not much fun these days, but a man's got to be curious what's worth this much to get out."

"That's not important," she answered bluntly. "What *is* important is that I have the money, and I'm willing to pay. Are you willing to *get* paid?"

He studied her with narrowed eyes, absentmindedly playing with the ring. Kerelle opened her senses further, trying to pick up any emotional projection. There was a chance he realized what she was, or at least guessed close enough to pose a danger. But if so, he didn't feel strongly enough to project - his thoughts were as closed off as his expression.

Ethics be damned, she needed to know if this was a trap. She reached out her powers and read his mind.

He was deeply, deeply suspicious. Big paydays didn't just

drop out of nowhere like this - this was either a corporate sting or something way too big to get involved in. But holy stars, the size of those gems. And they're real, he could spot counterfeit. And she'll pay *more*?

This was crazy, it was too much, she was obviously trouble and he didn't get this old in this business by taking stupid risks. But he'd pulled tough jobs before, and the payout would be pretty incredible, and stars knew staying on Zharal V waiting for the multigalactics to hit their endgame wasn't good for anyone's health.

Feeling mildly desperate, Kerelle made one last appeal to his avarice, adding a delicate brooch to the table. His eyes stayed on it for several seconds.

"I'll take the job," he answered gruffly, pocketing the gems. His better judgement was screaming so loud Kerelle could hear it now without trying.

She gave him her broadest smile and prayed he wouldn't change his mind. "Glad to hear it. I look forward to working together."

They agreed on a rendezvous time in two days, and Sandrel gave her directions to where his ship was docked. As she headed back to the base in a mix of terror and elation, Kerelle wasn't sure if it was her or the smuggler with more misgivings.

EIGHTEEN

THE ALARM'S soft beeping grew more insistent. Kerelle ignored it, staring up at the empty ceiling in her cramped sleeping quarters. It almost seemed too unreal to believe, that this was the last time she would wake up in this room, the last time she would wake up in her collar. If things went poorly, the last time she would wake up at all.

It felt like it should be different somehow, that something as momentous as her last morning in the PsiCorp should be somehow less mundane than the mornings preceding it. But here she was in the same room, the same alarm going off, the same terrible coffee awaiting her out in the mess hall. Somehow that made it all more surreal.

Kerelle finally turned off the alarm and swung herself out of bed. Surreal or not, it was here.

She dressed slowly and deliberately, each task taking on special import. Her jewelry collection, carefully secreted around her person where it was unlikely to be lost or damaged. The few clothes she had on hand that didn't have the SysTech logo somewhere on them, stuffed in her pack. Her dark hair, tied back and out of the way. Her PsiCorp jacket, slipped over her shoulders for likely the last time.

She'd scavenged a damaged lavatory mirror on one of their supply trips, and she now regarded herself in it dispassionately. Her normal self gazed back. Perhaps her brow was a bit more tense than it might usually be, but there was nothing to indicate she would be dead or free by the end of the day.

Whatever "free" even meant. The concept fluttered in her imagination, intangible and ill-defined but surely better than a future in the PsiCorp. It was what she wanted more than anything, what she was risking her life for. But as she stared back at herself with butterflies bouncing in her stomach, Kerelle realized she had no real idea what it would mean. What *did* it mean, to be psionic without the PsiCorp?

What did it mean to be Kerelle, without Senior Agent Evandra?

Almost unexpectedly, an answer surfaced in her mind. It would mean many things, surely, and she would have to learn what they were. But one thing it meant for *certain*: no matter how things ended today, win or lose, escape or die - she would never be complicit in another Elekar.

I will never be anyone's weapon. Not ever again.

The thought put a small smile on her lips as she scanned her sparse room one last time. A few of her things were still neatly piled, wherever there was space, but there was nothing of *her* that she was leaving behind.

She shut the door behind her.

NALEA'S VOICE cut insistently through the dull roar of the morning mess hall.

"Agent Evandra, I need to *speak* with you."

They'd gone over this a dozen times. Kerelle tried to project annoyance as she quirked an eyebrow and gestured for Nalea to continue.

"Agent Evandra, I am formally requesting to accompany the foraging team today. I'll stay out of the way."

"This isn't a field trip, Dr. Ambrel," she replied coolly. "And I'm not your babysitter."

"Yes," Nalea agreed with a gesture of impatience, "but there will be an entire team there, I'll be in little danger."

"Doctor, why in *stars* name would I let you come with us?"

Nalea shifted a bit in a show of reluctance. "There's a thing I want to look for. I have reason to believe it may be near where you're headed."

Kerelle folded her arms, brows raised. "A *thing*."

Nalea rolled her eyes in an exasperated gesture of *fine, you win*. "A thing that will help my research. A potential break-through. We can of course discuss patent royalty sharing with SysTech in recognition of your substantial assistance."

Kerelle gave her a quick nod. "Get your things, Doctor. We leave in 20 minutes. Don't get in the way."

Nalea took her at her word, and less than a half hour later their little group set out from the base. Kerelle led them towards the old StellarEye labs, her senses wide open. Usually, of course, she was trying to *avoid* ConEn. Today she was trying to find them.

Unease slithered down her spine. The squad was trusting her, and she was essentially leading them into an ambush. Kerelle tamped it down, trying to stay focused. For this to work her "death" had to be witnessed, and convincing. She'd do her best to protect the group from actual harm.

She caught the trail of a ConEn team not too far away - based on previous patterns, exactly where she was expecting them to be. She headed straight for them, until she could sense their presence only a short ways ahead. Almost in range for what came next.

Kerelle paused at the head of the squad, trying to keep her breath steady as they hurtled toward the point of no return. She could still shy away from it, go back to the base like nothing happened. Maybe they'd get a better chance later.

No. They wouldn't. It was now or never.

Kerelle took a deep breath, stepped past Nalea to scan the horizon, and exploded the world around them.

It was as big and flashy an explosion as she could manage, without actually hurting anyone. With a twinge of guilt she gave rest of the squad a telekinetic shove off their feet as if thrown by a shockwave. They'd think the explosion was bigger than it was. She and Nalea both dropped to the ground as dirt and debris rained all around the prone squad, and Kerelle wasn't sure if Nalea's scream was acting or genuine terror.

She had the ConEn team's attention now, and another quick blast near them sealed it. Shouts and shots rang out as their plan seemed to be working - both groups assumed the other had attacked. Kerelle lay as motionless against the shattered concrete, a small shield over herself and Nalea and larger-than-necessary clouds of dust and smoke swirling around to obscure the combatants from each other. But she didn't want a fight - she wanted a rout. For their own safety and hers, the SysTech squad needed to get out.

She hit them with the strongest compulsion she dared. *Run! They just killed a* Class 3, *you're outgunned,* run *you idiots!* It paid off - through the smoke, she heard the sounds of a retreat.

Kerelle tossed up the earth around her as if a grenade had gone off near her head, and rolled over to grab Nalea. With the smoke-choked chaos to screen them, they crept away. As soon as she dared, they started to run. Kerelle kept them both mentally shielded until they reached the darkened stairs to the lab. Once again, she shifted the debris behind them to better conceal the entrance.

Nalea paused to extract something from her pack, and a few

seconds later the portable light cube flickered to life in her hands. Under other circumstances Kerelle might have voiced her suspicions that Nalea had liberated it from one of the base's supply closets, but she was too jittery for banter. She might well be walking into her tomb.

Nalea's face was tense as well. "How long do we have before they come looking for you?"

"Probably not long," Kerelle answered tersely. "A few hours at most. They'll report my death, and Tallimau will see from my collar's status I'm alive. They'll probably assume I'm injured and the squad left me prematurely, but then they'll send a recovery team. We need to go fast."

"Well, that's the plan," Nalea muttered. She hurried Kerelle over to a vacant lab bench and started pulling items from her pack. A syringe, vials, more vials, a small hand-held med monitor. Kerelle's heart started to race as she watched this become more and more real. Fast but methodical, Nalea connected her to the little monitor, which confirmed her vitals with comforting little beeps. She rolled up Kerelle's other sleeve and swabbed down a spot on her arm.

Nalea paused then. "So I'm a researcher, not a medical doctor. Even if I *were* a medical doctor, these are shit conditions for a procedure like this. Even if I were a medical doctor and we were in a state of the art hospital, this is just a theory and there's zero proof it will work. There's a considerable chance you'll die." She met Kerelle's eyes. "I know we went over all this already, but this is your last chance to back out."

Kerelle forced herself to steadily return the gaze. "My last chance to back out was this morning," she asserted, proud that her voice did not waver. "Do it."

Nalea gave her a grim nod, and hit her with the first injection. The dampener.

Bravado aside, Kerelle was terrified, especially as the dampener began to take effect and she started to feel nauseous. This was real. It was happening. She tried to focus on her breathing as Nalea gave her the second injection. The suppressant - her powers suddenly fell away, and she barely kept from crying out. It was like a part of her had simply vanished. Her head was pounding, and her vision was beginning to blur. Was that the drugs or panic?

Too late for fear, too late for doubt. Even if she could back out now, she wouldn't. If she died on this lab bench, at least she would die trying. The monitor's beeps lost their reassuringly regular cadence.

Breathe. Breathe. Breathe. Kerelle focused on that simple task, that suddenly seemed so very challenging, and dimly registered the third injection as her vision began to fade.

NINETEEN

"DO you ever wonder what it would be like?"

"What what would be like?" Kerelle gazed from the corner of her eye at the boy beside her. Galhen stared up at the sky from their perch at the edge of the roof, his bright eyes fixed on those few stars with the fortitude to break through Tallimau's light-polluted skies. Her pulse raced at how close he sat to her.

"If we weren't here. Weren't psionic. If we were just random anybodies like them." He spread his arm wide to take in the glittering city beneath them. "What would we be doing?"

"Well, we probably wouldn't be on Tallimau, so we wouldn't be having this conversation, for one thing."

He laughed and turned to look at her. With an effort she met those sparkling eyes. Get it together, Kerelle, she groaned to herself. This is your friend. Don't make it weird. She'd always thought Galhen was pretty, of course, because he was, but there was something about being up here alone with him tonight that made it hard to think about anything else.

"No, I guess not," he agreed amiably. "I guess I would be back in Istel City going to secondary school like my brother was, studying for exams all the time. It's really weird to think about, actually - I'm almost the same age now that he was when I came to the PsiCorp. Balheren always seemed so old, and boring. Maybe it was all the exams."

She giggled a little. "Galhen, we have exams now."

Well yes, he said suddenly into her mind, but we get tested on useful things.

"Balheren wasn't?"

He grinned unrepentantly. "I have no idea. All I remember about his study notes is how angry he got when I drew space cruisers on them."

He propped himself up on an elbow as they laughed, and regarded her curiously. "Really though, Kerelle, what would you do if you could?"

She looked back up for a moment, turning the question over in her mind. It felt transgressive to even think about it, much less discuss it out loud. But she also felt safe up here on the roof, with just the sky above and the city below. Besides, Galhen had offered up his own transgression, the family and the life before that he was not supposed to talk about. She could offer hers too.

"I'd buy a ship and see the stars," she answered finally. "Fly from place to place meeting new people and seeing new worlds."

He tilted his head. "Isn't that what we'll do anyway when we finish training?"

"It would be my ship, though, and worlds I want to go to, not just wherever the company needs me. I...don't think I'll get to do a lot of sightseeing on assignments."

That cold pit in her stomach started to form again, same as it always did when she thought about what awaited her after they finished their training at the Academy. SysTech wasn't teaching her to perfect telekinetic explosions because they wanted her help with charity work.

Galhen sensed her change in mood and leaned over to meet her eyes again. "You'll do fine, Kerelle," he told her seriously. "And someday we'll find a way to see those stars." He gave her a half smile then, holding her gaze. "If I asked nicely, could I be on your crew?"

Kerelle sensed there were questions there, beyond the playful one he was asking. She answered all of them with a shy smile.

"Yes."

SHE HAD A HELL OF A HEADACHE.

The pounding in her head was the first thing to register as Kerelle drifted back to awareness, though it was followed closely by her roiling stomach. Her aching muscles soon put in their complaints as well, and Kerelle groaned slightly. Waking up seemed like a truly wretched idea, but someone was poking her insistently. As she began to come back to herself, another thought tugged at her, persistent but out of reach. There was a *reason* she was supposed to be awake, wasn't there?

She surrendered to inevitability and opened her eyes.

"Oh thank the burning stars," Nalea groaned. "You didn't die."

Kerelle blinked a few times and painfully levered herself into a sitting position, as her groggy mind tried to recall where they were and why she felt like she probably *ought* to have died. There was something strange as well, something she couldn't put her finger on -

Oh holy burning stars.

Her hands shook as she felt up to her throat. The collar was gone.

She burst into tears.

The great, shuddering sobs shook her whole body. It was if every feeling she'd ever had about the collar, about her duty, about her bondage to SysTech all melted down and erupted together. This was real. It happened. She could hardly process it.

Nalea fidgeted, clearly flustered by the sudden rush of tears. She busied herself with her equipment, efficiently packing it into her small bag.

"Right....so...clearly a lot to take in. It was a bit touch and go there for awhile, but your vitals have stabilized. You should probably go easy on your powers for a few days to let things heal. Maybe. We're in pretty uncharted territory." Nalea rubbed her brow. "It *kills* me that I can't publish a paper about this."

When Kerelle didn't respond, she cleared her throat. "But um, we need to meet your smuggler, and who knows how long we'll actually be safe here, so...if you could pull it together?"

Right. Work to do.

Well, shoving down her feelings to focus on the job was certainly something she knew how to do. Kerelle concentrated on her breathing then, forcing it to slow, to hold down those shivering sobs that still tried to wrack her frame. With effort she wrenched herself free of the flood of emotion, wrestled it into a mental compartment to deal with once this was over. She could fall apart later, after they were successful and safe. The tears dried.

She was still a bit wobbly as she tried to get to her feet. The nausea had passed, thank the stars, and the pain in her head receded to where it no longer felt like her skull would break itself apart, but she still felt weak and exhausted. *Fall apart later.* Another steadying breath.

Besides, Nalea was right. They had to move.

Nalea eyed Kerelle's shaky foray into standing upright. "Yeah... ideally you'd probably get a solid few days of rest after something like that, but hey." She shifted to offer Kerelle a shoulder to lean on. "Ideal situation and none of us would be here."

It was slow going at first, painfully so, as Kerelle leaned heavily on Nalea's smaller frame. But the upright movement seemed to help, and she found her feet by the time they'd reached the door. The door that she'd barricaded with debris before they started this. That had seemed like a better idea an hour ago.

"Well, so much for letting my powers rest," she muttered. Nalea gave her a small grimace but didn't argue.

It wasn't as bad as she feared. Tapping her powers set off

another twinge in her head, but it faded quickly, and everything seemed to be working normally. Gingerly she gave the debris a good shove, and it slid out of their way. Kerelle paused a moment to collect herself, and gave Nalea a quick nod. They stepped out of their erstwhile sanctuary into the dying sun.

A quick scan revealed no other humans nearby - SysTech and ConEn both must have retreated to lick their wounds. Kerelle prayed that luck would hold.

For now, the finishing touch. She shrugged out of her PsiCorp jacket and withdrew the nondescript hooded coat she'd worn to meet Sandrel from its place at the bottom of her field pack. As she finished fastening her makeshift disguise, Kerelle eyed her jacket with its SysTech logo and the distinctive open eye.

She wanted to shred it into a thousand pieces, but her better sense prevailed. Instead she added a few ragged rips and a smear of blood. *There. That looks like I took a direct hit from the shrapnel. Hopefully.* More convincing than leaving it in one piece, at least.

A thought occurred. "Nalea, what happened to my collar?"

The scientist gestured behind them. "Kicked it under one of those cabinets. I figured if they trailed you here and then found your snapped-off collar in the lab, this whole fake-your-death plan goes down the drain." She made a face. "You weren't hoping for a souvenir, were you?"

"If I ever see it again, it will be too soon." Kerelle tossed the jacket on a pile of rubble and reshouldered her pack. "I'm starting to feel that way about this whole moon, actually. Ready if you are?"

They started cautiously for the spaceport, the cover of night lending them its veil. Kerelle kept her aching senses as wide as she dared, alert for any presence that might endanger them. She sensed nothing, and they met no one, but Kerelle couldn't shake the terrible anticipation that SysTech would leap out to apprehend her at any moment. Their odyssey proved both uneventful and harrowing.

They kept their hoods up as they entered the more populated neighborhoods around the spaceport, and made it unchallenged to the docks. A little of the tightness in Kerelle's chest eased as she caught sight of Sandrel waiting where he said he'd be. He'd kept his end of the deal.

The smuggler was all business. "You have the payment?"

She nodded and pressed the heavy earrings into his hand. "Half now, half when we get there."

He nodded tersely and jerked a hand toward the open hatch. Hoping this wasn't a huge mistake, they followed him in.

The interior of the ship proved just as nondescript as its captain. It gave every appearance of an independent freighter, its functional but mismatched parts speaking to years of use and ad-hoc replacement on a modest income. From the furnishings to the instrument panels, everything seemed a bit worn but otherwise well-maintained. It looked like it could belong to any one of the hundreds of small, family-owned shipping firms that dotted the galaxy. It certainly did *not* look like the kind of ship that might run contraband, or skip a corporate blockade.

Kerelle had to hope that was an indication of Sandrel's skill at flying under the radar, and not that he was in over his head.

The captain gestured brusquely at the row of seats against the wall.

"Alright, sit down and strap in. This is pretty much guaranteed to be a bumpy ride. If you're going to vomit, do it on your stuff, not mine. We take off in five."

He took off, presumably towards the cockpit, leaving them to follow the brief directions. As Nalea strapped in, lips compressed, her second thoughts were written plainly across her face.

"Are we sure this guy is legit?" She hissed, leaning as far forward as the safety harness allowed.

Kerelle was about to reply when the engines sparked to life, accompanied by a distinctive humming noise as something else engaged. She recognized that sound, from missions that had taken her aboard SysTech spy ships. That was a stealth field generator - rare, expensive, and extremely illegal on civilian craft.

Well, that answered that question.

"He's legit," she replied. Nalea didn't look convinced, but then the purr of the engines changed tenor, the room around them began to move, and it was too late for either of them to reconsider.

At first the ascent was slow and smooth, as if they were gently gliding upward. Her only warning that that was about to change was another slight shift in engine noise before Sandrel took off like a shot. The vertical pressure was almost painful as they thrust unrelentingly upward, the engines' soft purr now a ferocious roar. Kerelle shut her eyes and tried to think of anything besides what they were doing right now. From beside her, she heard Nalea whimper.

Just as suddenly, it all went smooth and silent. They'd cleared atmosphere.

Kerelle eased her eyes open. Nalea kept hers tightly shut, fingers white-knuckled against the straps of her harness even as the ship settled.

"I can't tell if we're making progress or minutes away from disintegrating into the unforgiving vacuum of space." The words sounded as if she forced them out through clenched teeth.

"That we haven't disintegrated *yet* is a good sign," Kerelle offered. "We've cleared atmosphere. That means we got past the SysTech anti-aircraft guns."

Nalea didn't seem reassured. Kerelle wasn't terribly reassured either, but she felt like she owed it Nalea to pretend to be confident about this. As far as she knew, it was Nalea's first risky space maneuver. Kerelle hadn't been through that many risky space maneuvers herself, but at least her count was more than zero. That made her the old hand.

She was debating telling Nalea about the stealth field when the alarms suddenly screamed to life, and the ship jerked hard to one side. *So much for reassurance.*

The force of the turn threw them against their harnesses, then back again as they changed directions in a blink. Kerelle shamelessly threw her senses toward the cockpit to try to find out what was going on.

Sandrel's thoughts were loud enough she hardly had to try. *Shit shit shit I got too close to that one and now they have a read on us SHIT -*

Kerelle pulled back to herself, heart pounding. If the stealth field had failed, they were exposed before the whole ConEn fleet.

Nalea shrieked as they dropped low into a tight corkscrew. The ship pulled up again just as quickly before making a hard right that turned into a spin. Another hard twist, and a teeth-shaking boom as something hit the ship. Whatever that had been, Sandrel hadn't dodged it quickly enough.

That did it. If Kerelle was going to die, it wasn't going to be huddled helplessly strapped in a seat.

Nalea yelped as Kerelle released the harness, her eyes wide. "What are you *doing?!*"

"Anything I can," she barked in reply. "Stay here." Kerelle ignored the other woman's panicked protests as she carefully picked her way toward the cockpit. The ship banked hard again, and Kerelle had to stabilize herself with her telekinetics to keep from being thrown across the deck. Pain shot through her temples, reminding her that she wasn't exactly in top form.

Nalea has a point, this is probably really stupid.

She made it to the cockpit, the adrenaline lending her strength, but hung back once she reached the door. Sandrel's fancy flying was all that kept ConEn from blasting them into dust, and she didn't want to distract him.

Sandrel himself was perched on the edge of the pilot's chair, outwardly calm, though his knuckles were white against the controls. He threw the ship into another evasive maneuver, and Kerelle had to stabilize herself again as he sped fearlessly through a narrow gap between two ConEn cruisers. Two of many. She could see how Sandrel had accidentally brushed too close - the orbit around Zharal V was blanketed with enemy vessels.

Another dive to avoid a missile, a graceful arc over a larger ship. Sandrel's overriding thought projected loudly enough to pick up without trying.

Just a bit further. Just a bit further out and we can make a clean jump.

An alarm spiked and he banked hard, but not fast enough. The entire ship shook with a sickening boom as they were hit again. *FUCK*, she heard from Sandrel, *I can't shake this asshole.* Kerelle listened a bit harder and got a visual - a small, agile fighter craft, one of several launched from one of the cruisers. Sandrel had been able to lose the others, but this one's pilot was very good, and his nimble craft gave him an advantage.

This she could help with. Kerelle braced herself in the hallway, hoping they wouldn't go into any more corkscrews while she was distracted. With a deep breath she threw her senses out as far as she could, gritting her teeth against the intensifying pain in her head. There was Sandrel, utterly focused on his task, unaware of her lurking presence. There was Nalea, sobbing helplessly alone in the harness and wondering if the end would hurt. And there, there at the very edge of her range. There was the ConEn pilot, the buzz of victory beginning to rise in his veins as he closed in on his quarry.

Kerelle paused, and time seemed to pause with her. She could kill him from here, most likely. She could try to hit his emergency eject, or she could try to smash his vidport and let the vacuum rend it asunder. She felt it out with her power, ready to blow a hole in the little craft and consign its pilot to the frozen void.

No one's weapon. Surely she could do this without anyone else having to die.

Kerelle let the craft go and returned to the pilot. He was lining up another shot on them now, they didn't have space to evade, he would end this. Her pulse raced as she waited for him to lock on, prepare to fire...

She shoved the false vision into his mind with all her might, the ersatz sight of Sandrel suddenly reversing course and speeding towards him. The pilot drew back startled, dropping his target and missing their sudden shift in trajectory. Sandrel had the opening he needed.

He brought them out of a spin and shot toward clear space. *Almost there, almost there...*

The sensors lit up like a carnival. Kerelle couldn't suppress a gasp as dozens of ships dropped out of orbit around them, the view screen suddenly bright with laser fire. The SysTech fleet ignored their tiny vessel as it moved in aggressively to engage the ConEn ships.

One way or another, it seemed the dispute over Zharal V was about to be resolved.

Sandrel didn't stay to watch. A final dive to avoid a large SysTech ship, and he gunned it past the incoming fleet to open space. Sandrel's fingers flew over the controls, and she hardly had time to prepare before a bright light flashed through the viewscreen and the battle around them dissolved.

It was silent then, the vidports showing only a soft unfocused glow. The unnatural calm of hyperspace settled around the ship like a comforting embrace, and bore them safely away.

TWENTY

SOMETHING JOLTED HER AWAKE. Kerelle stared confused at the strange ceiling for several minutes before her mind caught up with her surroundings. Her hand strayed involuntarily back up to her bare throat. It was real.

She didn't have time to ponder her altered reality, however. Something had woken her, and as she thought back carefully she recognized what the sensation had been. Their ship had dropped from hyperspace, more abruptly than it should have.

As much as she wanted to curl up and go back to sleep, she probably ought to investigate that.

Kerelle got painfully to her feet. Her headache had receded after the previous day's exertions, but she still felt a dull ache in all her muscles, as if she'd run for hours. *Maybe someday I'll actually get those solid several days of rest Nalea recommended.* The way things were going, it didn't seem promising.

She met Nalea herself in the corridor. The scientist didn't look like she'd had a particularly restful night either. Dark circles beneath her eyes underscored an expression of deep concern.

"That felt bad," Nalea said without preamble. "What happened?"

"Well, I was asleep," Kerelle noted, "but it felt like we just dropped out of hyperspace. Hard."

Nalea's frown deepened. "Come to think of it, Captain Marene didn't exactly relax after we got away from Zharal. Do you think there's something wrong with the ship?"

A knot of worry coalesced in her gut that that was exactly the case. But she only said, "We won't find out by standing here."

They found Sandrel grim-faced in the cockpit. He flicked a switch in the control board and turned to face them, his features set in a coolly professional mask.

"So I'm sure you noticed we dropped out of hyper," he told them briskly. "We took a lot of damage getting past that block-ade, and unfortunately the hyperdrive took one of the hits."

"Is that as bad as it sounds?" Kerelle tried to keep her voice steady and unconcerned. Nalea had gone ice-white, and Kerelle owed it to her to keep it together.

"It's certainly not good. The drive is failing, and we're going to need to stop somewhere for repairs. I'd hoped to get us to Palhee on the current drive, but the readings I'm getting aren't promising."

He delivered this news in the same calm and professional tone, but Kerelle could sense a clenched tension behind it. With a creeping sense of dread, she asked the obvious question.

"Is there anywhere nearby we can get those repairs?"

"Nearby, yes. We were near an inhabited world when the hyperdrive started sputtering. I dropped us out rather than risk the drive failing mid-jump. We should be able to make it to Kalnis in about a week on the engines."

He didn't sound terribly happy about it.

Kerelle kept her voice level. "I'm not familiar with Kalnis. Is there a problem?"

"It's not a place I would recommend *becoming* familiar with. We'll get in, get what we need, and get out."

That didn't sound promising at all. But Sandrel clearly didn't want to elaborate, and Nalea was already looking like she might be ill at any moment. Kerelle didn't want to add to her distress by finding out just how bad the situation might be. She'd get more information out of Sandrel later, and if the hyperdrive was truly that damaged, they didn't have any alternatives anyway.

So for now she only agreed, and led the other woman back to the passenger cabins where they'd slept. When the door swished shut behind them, Nalea sat down hard on the edge of the bed.

"If it's just a matter of stopping someplace nearby for repairs, why does Captain Marene seem so on edge?"

Because the place we're stopping is almost as dangerous as not stopping at all, was Kerelle's guess, but from her expression Nalea had deduced that as well, and was hoping Kerelle might give her a different answer.

"I'm sure Captain Marene knows what he's doing," Kerelle tried to reassure her. "And if things go badly, well," she shrugged and gave what she hoped was a confident smile. "You have me."

Nalea glanced over her shoulder, though several walls were between them and the cockpit. "About that. Does he know...?"

Kerelle shook her head. "Only that we're paying a lot for transport. I'm sure he's put together that we aren't on a pleasure cruise, but he doesn't know anything about...me. The fewer people who know, the better for all of us, I think."

"No arguments here." Nalea stretched and looked around the sparse cabin. "I guess I'm getting time to compile those research notes after all."

SANDREL TENDED to avoid his passengers and keep to himself in the cockpit. Kerelle wanted to respect his space, but after trying unsuccessfully to catch him in the mess or a corridor, she gave up and headed into their pilot's sanctum.

He didn't look thrilled to see her there, but he greeted her politely nonetheless. Kerelle got right down to business.

"So I gathered yesterday that the location of our detour is not someplace you'd prefer to stop at."

"It wouldn't be my first choice," he agreed. "But we need repairs, and Kalnis is where we can get them. It isn't the first time I've been there. Don't concern yourself, we'll get to Palhee just fine." His guard was up, however, and that tension was back, radiating at the edges of her senses. She was briefly tempted to just read his mind to get her answer, but no - this wasn't an emergency, and there was no life-or-death justification for rooting around his head uninvited. No matter how badly she wanted to know.

She tried again. "All the same, I'd like to know what to expect. I'm not the panicking type, if that's your concern."

"That's appreciated." There was a sardonic note in his otherwise mild response. He sighed and shifted in his seat to face her more fully.

"Look, Kalnis is a rough town. The whole sector is infested with pirates, and most of them are based on the planet's surface. At any time there are multiple pirate gangs vying for control, and they don't hesitate to start shooting at whatever crosses their path. That's assuming someone makes it there at all - there's an asteroid field nearby that those same pirates like to use as cover for ambushing ships. Kalnis isn't someplace you want to go if you've got any other options."

He gestured at the great yawning void of open space, gliding silently past the vidports. "But *our* only other option was to pray to the stars that the hyperdrive didn't fail and incinerate us on reentry, or drop us into an empty patch years of realspace travel away from anything. And since I've never found the stars to be particularly responsive to prayers, we're taking our chances with Kalnis."

Kerelle nodded resignedly. Well, she did ask.

"Is there anything we can do?"

"Keep quiet and follow directions," he answered firmly. "I try to avoid this whole sector, but I *have* had to occasionally visit Kalnis on business. I know where to get what we need and we won't have to linger long. If we don't draw attention to ourselves, everything should be fine."

Kerelle sensed he didn't quite believe those words himself, but there wasn't much any of them could do except hope that they were true.

IT WAS A LONG WEEK. The ship was reasonably comfortable, but as Sandrel commented sharply, it was not a pleasure barge. It provided little in the way of entertainment to while away the long hours in space. After she'd caught up on sleep, Kerelle found herself at loose ends.

She tried using the time to think about what would happen after they eventually reached this Palhee, but the entire concept still seemed so unreal that she had trouble envisioning what their next moves could look like. Finally she gave up, and heaved herself off her small bed to seek out some company.

Sandrel remained polite and professional, but had also made it clear he preferred not to be disturbed by his passengers. So it was that her footsteps took her down to Nalea's cabin instead.

Nalea, at least, was making good use of their time. True to her word, she was immersed in her research notes on the collars, and it took her several moments to notice Kerelle was there.

"What are you working on?" Kerelle asked her curiously.

Encouraged that she hadn't been immediately thrown out, she seated herself lightly on the edge of the bed.

"Nothing now, if you're going to interrupt me," Nalea groused, but there was no rancor behind the words. She indicated a sheet of diagrams and equations Kerelle couldn't identify. "I'm trying to work out a better way to remove the collars, preferably one that doesn't involve temporarily killing whoever we're trying to save."

"I thought you said they don't come off, otherwise...?"

"I said they weren't *designed* to come off, and that I didn't know any other way to do it. That's not the same as saying it's not possible."

She pointed at one of the diagrams. "A lot of the function is tied into the external control mechanism." She clarified: "The thing that lets your handlers turn them on."

"It's a card," Kerelle told her. "About the size of a payment card. I've only actually *seen* them a few times, but the Director at Tallimau has one that controls mine. Obviously when Senator Dalanva bought Galhen, they gave her a card that controls his." She couldn't keep the venom out of her voice.

"Well, from what I can look at here, the cards seem to regulate a lot of things besides just the kill switch." Kerelle winced a bit at the bald description, but Nalea didn't notice. "It's possible that if we had a control card available, we might be able repurpose it for removal." She shrugged. "Or we might not. This is all just theory unless I can get a working card to run some tests."

Nalea looked up at her somewhat balefully. "If by some miracle we all survive this, and if by some *other* miracle I get a chance to publish on it without risking my neck, you owe me your agreement to be cited as a case study."

Kerelle didn't get a chance to reply. Instead, Sandrel's voice cut tersely across the intercom.

"Strap in. We've got company."

———————

AS THEY RAN down the hallway towards the safety harnesses, the noise from the proximity alarm grew louder. The ship lurched alarmingly, nearly throwing both women across the floor. Nalea reached the seats and quickly pulled down the harness. Kerelle didn't slow down, instead sprinting the last small way to the cockpit. She wasn't going to sit helplessly by this time.

Sandrel gave a her a quick glance as she burst in, his mouth tight. He pulled them up quickly to avoid something and she had to grab the copilot seat to avoid falling. Kerelle caught a quick glance of a large vessel in the viewscreen, bearing down on them with alarming speed. Even in her brief look, she'd seen the skulls painted on the other ship's exterior. They weren't even *pretending* not to be pirates.

"Strap *in!*" He shouted irritably. He banked left again. "We have to get out of here!"

"I want to help!"

Sandrel practically growled back at her, his eyes never leaving the screen. "I don't have time for this. Get to the gunnery if you can shoot straight, otherwise *get your ass strapped in.*"

Kerelle didn't wait for any further instructions. She turned and sped the short distance to the gunnery turret, glad she'd noted its location in her earlier wanderings around the ship. She scaled the ladder in a few leaps and hooked herself into the gunner's harness.

The ship spun wildly again as Sandrel continued evasive maneuvers against their larger opponent. Even Kerelle could tell, however, that the ship was not as responsive as it had been leaving Zharal V, and a dull *thunk* against the walls underscored that the damaged vessel had lost some of its quick maneuverability. They'd have a hard time simply outrunning the pirates.

Time to put those guns to use.

The gunnery offered a vidport as well, albeit smaller than the one in the cockpit. That was fine - she only needed to see what she was trying to hit. Kerelle was not well trained in ship weapons, but it didn't seem complicated to fire the guns - and anyway, the guns themselves were only secondary.

She got off a shot against the other ship, a sharp retort echoing from the gun she sat above. It was absorbed by the pirate's shields with no visible damage, but she had an idea now what they could do. She fired the gun again, and this time used its loud arc as cover to hammer her telekinetics against the area her shot would land. The effect was much more satisfying.

Kerelle found herself grinning as she lined up the next one. Let the pirates wonder what the hell this little ship's gun was packing.

Boom. Boom. Crash. She didn't hold back, channeling her frustration with the last few months into a series of assaults against their encroaching enemy. It was a big ship, solid and heavy and well-constructed, and she couldn't exactly punch holes in its vidports like she'd considered with the lightweight ConEn fighter. But she put dents in its sides, and when Sandrel thrust them upward to give her a brief top-down view of their opponent, she threw everything she had against its primary gun. It gave a viscerally satisfying *crunch*, and the barrel cracked.

The pirates fell back then, and Sandrel took off like a shot away from them. The other ship faded to a speck in her viewscreen.

"Not bad for a corporate princess," Sandrel's voice crackled over the intercom. "If I didn't know better, I'd think someone installed a Fury cannon down there when I wasn't looking. I'm not going to ask where you learned to shoot like that."

Kerelle couldn't help a smile, even if his guess as to her origins hit a bit too close to the mark.

"Always happy to help. Does this mean I don't have to strap

down in the passenger quarters next time the proximity alarm goes off?"

"Let's hope there *isn't* a next time. I'm taking us down into the main Kalnis docks in about an hour. Now we just hope those pirates don't have any friends waiting once we're down there."

TWENTY-ONE

EVEN FROM THE AIR, Kalnis was a teeming, derelict mess. Here and there were the shells of grand buildings, indicating that perhaps things had once been better - or at least that someone with investment money had believed they might *get* better. Judging by the age and condition of those buildings now, any such hopes had long since fled. They dropped down over a sea of rickety walls and broken windows to touch ground at a drab concrete field surrounded by razor wire.

They were met at the landing pad by a shifty man in a worn port authority uniform. Sandrel paid him the requested docking fee, then reached into his jacket to count out another two hundred credits. The port worker pocketed it with a nod and moved on.

Sandrel caught Kerelle's questioning glance as he returned to the ship.

"First amount is the docking fee we pay to land here. The second one is the 'security fee,' which is a nice way of saying the bribe that makes sure the ship is *still* here when we get back." He explained this nonchalantly without having to be asked;

Kerelle's gunner performance had apparently elevated her in Sandrel's opinion.

Sandrel turned to regard them both. "Doc, are you sure you want to stay with the ship?"

Nalea gave a small nod. She'd been quiet since they got their first good look at Kalnis, and her second thoughts about the entire venture were written plainly across her face.

"All right then," he said. "Keep everything locked up, stay out of sight and don't answer the door. We paid our bribe to keep the ship from being stolen, but it never hurts to be extra careful, especially here. We'll be back as soon as we have the parts we need." Nalea only nodded again and drew back further into the ship. Kerelle felt a twist of worry at leaving her, but locked inside the ship was probably far safer than roaming the streets.

Up close, Kalnis was even worse off than it looked in the air. Garbage carpeted the claustrophobic streets, with scattered piles of pungent refuse that spoke to a lack of accessible sanitation. The uneven sidewalks were hemmed in by crumbling concrete block towers, many with plywood shanties built around them like vines beginning to choke a tree - though she hadn't seen a tree since they broke atmosphere. Most people they passed hurried about their business, carefully not looking at anyone. Those that didn't were the clusters of rough-looking individuals who leaned against walls here and there, watching the passerby like sharks sizing up a school of fish.

Sandrel walked with brisk purpose and no sign of fear, and Kerelle followed suit. All the same, she brushed those they passed with telepathic encouragement that there was nothing about her and Sandrel worth noticing. As the smuggler had said, it never hurt to be extra careful.

True to his word, Sandrel knew where they were going, and he led them unerringly to a battered storefront in a small cluster of merchants that passed for a shopping center. With reinforced bars over their windows and heavy chains to secure their doors, it seemed more to Kerelle that the shops were huddled for mutual defense.

She waited quietly to the side while Sandrel negotiated for what they needed. She could be of no help fixing the ship, but she didn't intend to stand idly by. Kerelle kept her senses open for anyone in their vicinity who might be trouble. She'd done a good job on the way in though, or else Sandrel had, because she sensed no one who had taken note of them. So far so good.

Sandrel briskly shook hands with the proprietor and credits changed hands, and soon they were back in those filthy streets with several small boxes stowed in his pack. Kerelle marveled that their survival could be contained in such little things, but it was probably for the best they didn't have to visibly carry them.

She kept up her mental shield of anonymity as they made their way back to the dock, and to her relief they passed back into the bleak little shipyard without incident. Now all they had to do was install the parts and leave this wretched world behind them. There was just one problem.

The ship was gone.

***

SANDREL WHIRLED around at the empty berth, charging toward the nearest port worker. "What the hells is this? I paid the security fee, where in the *burning void* is my ship?"

The other man wouldn't meet his eyes and ducked away towards the small office area. Kerelle's eyes widened as she picked up the imminent attack.

"Sandrel!" She yelped, shifting position so their backs faced each other, "Trouble!"

She'd scarcely said it when trouble burst in, guns blazing.

She had a shield up in seconds, though she dropped it again just as quickly after the initial volley. Sandrel pulled her down beside him behind a haphazard stack of crates, swearing incoherently as he returned fire.

There were a half dozen of them, and she didn't dare use her telekinetics in front of so many witnesses. Instead Kerelle hit the closest attacker with telepathic equivalent of a slap across the face. He was startled into dropping his gun, and Sandrel took him down with a clean shot. He kept firing and clipped a second one in the shoulder. The man staggered back.

Thinking quickly, Kerelle gave him a mental shove to throw him further off-balance. His foot brushed the gun the other man had dropped, and she streaked it across the room towards them as if he'd kicked it in his stumbling. She snatched it up and fired.

Sandrel spared her a second's glance and went back to firing. Kerelle's aim was not as good as Sandrel's, but she kept up the pressure with a barrage of shots. Their opponents were down to three, but they were wary now, and spread out carefully to present smaller targets.

She felt the intent almost before the action, which registered just as a tiny clink sounded on the crate above them.

"Grenade!" She shrieked, and threw herself to the side. Sandrel did the same almost immediately, and had scarcely cleared the crates when their erstwhile shelter exploded into a rain of splinters.

It was a high-stakes dodging game then, as the remaining thugs opened fire. Sandrel took out one more with a well-placed hit, but from his grunt of pain he wasn't fast enough to dodge the other. Kerelle hit one with another telepathic slap, taking advantage of the momentary confusion to finish her. Realizing he was suddenly outnumbered, the final thug ran for the exit. He didn't make it.

Sandrel wasted no time. Almost before the sudden stillness could register, he'd leapt the flimsy counter that delineated the dock's offices, and had the port worker by his shirt.

"What was *that*," he growled, giving the trembling man a shake for emphasis, *"and where is my ship?"*

The port worker's fear battered at Kerelle like a physical assault. She closed her eyes briefly, upping her mental shields to tamp it down.

"I'm sorry," he was stammering. "I'm really sorry. But the security fee doesn't count against the Ash and Bones."

"Is that who *they* were?" Sandrel jerked his head dismissively at the bodies sprawled across the shipyard floor.

The man nodded nervously. "Big group of them showed up a little after you left, said you'd crossed the Ash and Bones and you'd pay the price. Took the ship and left that lot behind to wait for you."

Kerelle and Sandrel exchanged glances. It looked like those pirates they'd fought off had friends on the surface after all.

Kerelle was afraid to ask the next question. "Did anyone see a blonde woman leaving the ship?" It seemed unlikely Nalea would have wandered off on her own, but...

Her fears were realized as the port worker nodded without meeting her gaze. "They hauled her out when they took the ship. Last I saw they shoved her into their transport in restraint cuffs."

The pirates had Nalea. The thought sent a queasy spiral through her gut.

Sandrel dropped the terrified dock attendant, who tore off immediately for the shipyard's exit. He turned to her, his cool, businesslike mask back in place.

"We need to move before this Ash and Bones group checks in with their friends here. Stay close and we'll talk when we get there."

She did, keeping a hand near her purloined weapon as she followed him through the winding streets. He led her on a careful journey through backstreets and alleys, doubling back a few times for good measure. Sandrel stayed grimly silent through their trek, though she could sense his tight worry - and pain, now that the adrenaline was wearing off from their confrontation with the pirate squad. The shot seemed to have grazed his shoulder, but Kerelle noted the blood beginning to trickle down his jacket.

They finally ended at a worn hotel. The proprietor didn't look at them as they entered, only rattled off the price of a room and handed over a key as Sandrel deposited a handful of credits on the counter. Kerelle got the impression he preferred not to know who he rented to.

When they were safely ensconced in their room - or at least as safe as they were likely to get on Kalnis - Kerelle finally let out her breath.

"We have to save Nalea," she blurted bluntly.

"Yes," Sandrel responded, the familiar sardonic tone back in his voice. "I'm rather fond of my ship, too." He stripped off his jacket and shirt and gave his shoulder a critical look, then turned to the suite's meager selection of towels. With a faint tsk of disgust, he selected the least disreputable of the bunch and started wetting it down.

"We're going to need a *plan*, though," he continued as he cleaned the graze wound. He batted away Kerelle's hand as she tried to help. "Judging by the reaction of that guy at the docks, I don't think anyone's going to just give us directions to wherever the Ash and Bones keep their stolen goods."

Sandrel finished cleaning off the blood and to her surprise produced a small vial of dermal regen gel from his jacket, which he carefully applied to the tear in his flesh with a finesse that indicated it wasn't his first time. That he had dermal regen gel stashed in his jacket pocket, apparently as a matter of course, made Kerelle wonder how eventful his jobs tended to be.

Unease twisted in her as she considered his words. She could locate Nalea much more quickly with telepathy, but it would mean confessing to Sandrel just who he had agreed to transport. Not that she wouldn't do that to save Nalea, but if they had any other options...

Mistaking her expression, Sandrel put a reassuring hand on her arm. "They probably won't hurt your friend," he told her seriously. "She's way more valuable alive and unharmed, either to sell or to ransom. And frankly, you two seem like someone would *pay* your ransom."

"No one I'd want to see," Kerelle answered honestly. Director Cafora's paternal smile and hard eyes rose in her mind, and she suppressed a shiver.

"Not even to get away from pirates, hm?" Sandrel raised his eyebrows and gave her a frank look. "Whatever you two are running from, Fury, it must be considerable."

She didn't bother to deny it. "All the more reason to move quickly, before the pirates can sell her. One way or another."

"I agree," he told her, holding up a placating hand, "but it'll take time to figure out where she's being held."

Time Nalea might not have, she realized. Perhaps Sandrel was right and the pirates would simply ransom her to Olstenfel... or maybe they would sell her into slavery, or kill her in revenge for the ship's earlier escape. Kerelle could not be as sanguine as Sandrel.

Which meant it was time to take a calculated risk.

"Sandrel," she said softly, forcing herself to meet his eyes, "I can find them faster."

He looked at her quizzically, a touch of suspicion coloring his gaze. *Here goes nothing.*

She lifted a thin pillow from the hotel's narrow bed and floated it gently across the room, coming to a light rest in her hand. Sandrel's warm-hued skin went pale.

Whatever regard she might have gained in their previous adventures vanished like mist in the sun. Instead he stared at her like she was a coiled snake who might strike at any moment; Kerelle wasn't sure he was aware he'd taken a step back. When

Sandrel finally found his voice again, it was a hiss of anger covering for fear.

"What the hell *is* this?"

Kerelle was committed now, and she might as well go the whole way. She opened the top of her jacket, exposing the pale ring at her throat where the collar had rested for 25 years.

"It's this," she said simply. "You're right. I *am* running from something considerable."

"I didn't sign up for this," he retorted, an angry flush blooming in his cheeks. "There's not enough money in the *universe* to sign up for this."

"You didn't sign up for pirates, either, but here we are. Things aren't going to plan for either of us." His jaw tightened, and she knew she was losing him. Kerelle sighed deeply and tried again.

"Sandrel. SysTech thinks I'm dead." *Hopefully.* She kept that part to herself. "They aren't chasing me, aren't chasing *you*. That woman risked her life and her career to help me escape, and we are *not* leaving her to the pirates."

She floated the pillow again, returning it to its place on the bed. "I'm a telekinetic and a telepath. I can use my powers to find Nalea and the ship, and help us escape with them. But I need you to calm down and work with me."

He gestured angrily at himself. "Can't you just *make* me work with you? How do I even know you haven't been pulling my strings this whole time?"

"That's not actually possible," she told him. "It's not like in the movies. Telepaths can't control people's minds. I can give someone a telepathic suggestion, and maybe they'll think it's their own idea. Sometimes I can influence emotions, and push someone to feel something more or less. But it works best when it's something they expect to see, or something they might do anyway. The further removed a suggestion is from reality, the more chance their mind will realize it's wrong."

She spread her hands. "Yes, if I had no sense of ethics, I could try to make you think you wanted to help. I could try to make you think that you wanted your ship back more than you didn't want to deal with me. Maybe it would work, for a short time, but your mind would fight me, and we probably wouldn't get six steps outside until you realized this wasn't what you wanted at all.

"Sandrel, I'm not threatening you, I'm not compelling you. I'm *asking* you, one person to another, for your help. We got into this together, and staying together will make it much easier to get out."

He took several deep breaths, turning over what she said. Finally he met her gaze, face tight.

"All right. We find your friend and my ship. We get to Palhee as agreed, you get the hell off my ship, I never see you again."

"Deal," she answered firmly. They could solve the transport problem later, when Nalea's life was not in imminent peril. It was enough just to get to Palhee.

Sandrel's frown remained in place, his fierce emotions radiating at her senses. Mistrust, displeasure, and a considerable amount of fear... but she didn't sense any duplicity, or any indication he was considering selling her out to SysTech. She didn't realize she'd been nervous about that until the thin coil of relief eased over her shoulderblades.

She stuck her hand out, and after a flash of hesitation he shook it. It was time to get to work.

TWENTY-TWO

THEIR HOTEL ROOM may have been cramped and threadbare, but it offered relative quiet and privacy. Kerelle gingerly seated herself on the edge of the bed, hoping any vermin it held were currently otherwise occupied. Sandrel leaned against the wall, his cool mask back in place and firmly concealing the tense discomfort that pushed against her senses. She took a few deep breaths to center herself, closed her eyes, and opened herself to Kalnis.

In its own way, the psychic landscape of Kalnis was as bad as Zharal V under siege. The wretched city was choked with the misery, fear, and despair of its inhabitants, and for a moment it threatened to overwhelm her. She gritted her teeth and pushed it back, searching amidst the sea of suffering for the spark of Nalea. It was easier this time than it had been on Zharal. Now that she was better acquainted with Nalea herself, Kerelle knew what she was looking for.

There. She picked up a trace of Nalea's energy, distant but vital, and almost cried with relief. Now that she'd located Nalea alive, Kerelle could admit how much she'd been afraid she was already dead.

She opened her eyes to meet Sandrel's wary gaze.

"I've got her. I'm too far to pinpoint her exactly, but I have a general location. We'll know more as we get closer to where she is."

"And where is that, exactly?"

Kerelle thought back to the flashes she'd seen from other minds on her way to Nalea. "I think it's some kind of compound. Your ship is probably there too."

"*Probably* there?" He sounded mildly indignant.

"Ships don't have thoughts for me to pick up," she replied dryly. "Judging by what I *did* pick up from people in the vicinity, the compound is the main base of operations for this Ash and Bones group. They'll probably have your ship there with them."

Sandrel's frown deepened. "Breaking into a cartel base and escaping with the Doc, my ship and our lives aren't great odds."

"They'll be better if we don't get caught," she replied. "I can probably get us in without attracting attention. The bulk of my field experience is not in stealth, but it's not my first time, and in any case I want to avoid any flashy displays of psionics. SysTech thinks I'm dead and I'd like to keep it that way."

"Getting *in* isn't the part I'm worried about," Sandrel muttered, but he didn't seem to have any better ideas. He looked her up and down. "What exactly can you *do*, anyway?"

Kerelle smiled tightly. "Enough."

KERELLE HAD SEEN a cartel base or two - as a negotiator's muscle when it served SysTech's interest to work with the underworld, and as an assailant when it did not. In her admittedly limited experience, they tended to follow one of two aesthetics. There were the delusions-of-grandeur types, who styled themselves after parliaments or corporate headquarters as if to confer legitimacy on their operations by sheer weight of the trappings of authority. Then there were the ones who wielded their illegal status as a club of intimidation, and presented their fortresses as a structural ode to nihilism. It did not surprise her at all that the Ash and Bones were the second type.

It did indeed seem to be a compound of some size, ringed by thick concrete walls topped with razor wire - and, Kerelle noted with disgust, evidence of the Ash and Bones' namesake. There were no hints to whom the blackened skeletal limbs woven into the fence had once belonged to, but presumably they were others who had incurred the pirate gang's displeasure.

"Charming," Sandrel murmured from beside her. They were concealed for the moment in an alleyway that offered a reasonably unobstructed view of the compound's gates. Now that she had them in her sight, Kerelle rather wished for a bit of obstruction.

"It certainly doesn't make me regret not surrendering to them in space," she responded in a whisper. "This is the place, though. I can sense Nalea inside."

"Hopefully in one piece." Sandrel tore his gaze away from the gruesome walls. "So how does the famous PsiCorp plan to get inside?"

"I'm not PsiCorp any more," she answered firmly. "But back when I was, I did this kind of thing a time or too. We need to find someone who's supposed to be going in and out, who's unlikely to draw much attention inside."

She didn't have to cast around very far to find the cleaning staff. Every organization had them, and every organization underestimated just how much access they had inside.

She led Sandrel quietly around towards the side of the compound, careful to keep up a low-level aura discouraging any passerby from taking note of them. The last thing they needed was a local hoping to curry favor with the gang by reporting the suspicious pair loitering around the walls.

She mentally sighed in relief as they turned a corner and

caught sight of a service entrance. The door was smaller, less imposing, and thankfully lacking in human remains. It was also propped open as a small group of people pushed carts laden with cleaning supplies in and out. Even better - she had been fully prepared to wait in the shadows all day precisely for this to happen.

"That's how we're getting in," she told Sandrel. "Stick close."

A quarter-hour later, they were pushing an appropriated supply cart in through the small door, wrapped in the drab brown aprons of the compound's serving staff. Kerelle kept them shielded with anonymity as tightly as she could as they passed inside, but the single bored-looking guard didn't even look up as they went by. Score one for the subtle approach.

Kerelle kept pushing her cart forward as they entered a large building and started down a long hall, hoping Sandrel would keep following quietly until they found a spot to reconvene. She was gaining a new appreciation for working with other telepaths on missions like this.

Telepath he might not be, but Sandrel was hardly an amateur either. He kept up silently, giving every impression he was supposed to be there, until Kerelle saw their opportunity in a small alcove. They ducked inside.

"That went well," she noted quietly. "I don't sense alarms from any of the guards. I think we're in clean."

Sandrel nodded. "On to the next problem then. I know you're worried about the Doc, but we'll have an easier time with the getaway if we find my ship before we break her out."

As much as Kerelle wanted to rescue Nalea without delay, she knew he was right. If all went according to plan they'd slip out with Nalea as quietly as they slipped in, but they hadn't had an abundance of success with "going to plan" lately.

"All right. I'll try to get a bead on anyone who works near vehicle storage. Hopefully the ship is somewhere easy to get out of."

She pushed the supply cart deeper into the alcove and extracted a pair of buckets. "We can probably leave the cart here and just switch to these. We'll still look like we're part of the cleaning staff, but without the hassle of lugging that thing around."

"I had no idea psionic defenses involved so many disguises," Sandrel noted somewhat dryly. He picked up his bucket anyway.

"Like I said, the more someone is expecting to see something, the easier it is to convince them they're seeing it." Kerelle hefted her new burden. "Whatever happens, we just keep walking and carrying these buckets like we have every reason to be in here carrying these buckets. I'll take care of the rest."

She took advantage of their current seclusion to do another telepathic scan of their surroundings, this time looking for thoughts that might lead to their ship. It was easier than she was expecting - there was a hanger not that far from them, and it was well-staffed.

Kerelle kept up the aura of nothing-to-see-here as they made their way down the corridor. They passed numerous groups of pirates, most in the raucously rowdy mood that indicated intoxicants had been flowing. Whether due to her shield or the inherent invisibility of their disguises, however, none took note of Sandrel and Kerelle.

Still, she took note of *them*. If this plan went sideways, they'd have a lot of pirates to get through before they could escape.

The hangar itself wasn't vast, but it was well-populated. Kerelle recognized the larger ship that had attacked them in orbit, silent and looming near the mouth of the bay. Smaller ships surrounded it like a litter of perverse kittens. The makeshift fleet was a mishmash of types and origins - she saw a range of freighter models, a larger transport ship, even something that looked like it may have been a military fighter craft. All had been heavily painted with the pirates' favorite skull motif. Kerelle wondered how many of the ships' original owners were on the wall outside.

Sandrel's ship was near the edge of the collection. The pirates clearly intended to come back to it - mechanics' tools were scattered across a hydraulic lift near the entrance - but for the moment it seemed unattended.

"Glad we got here before they started redecorating," Sandrel muttered darkly. Kerelle could only nod her agreement.

"At least it's a straight shot out the hangar. But…" she trailed off, not wanting to voice it but knowing it couldn't be avoided. "With the hyperdrive broken are we really going to get far?"

"It'll complicate things," he acknowledged. "But I didn't get here by not being able to handle complications. If we can make it into orbit, we can lose them in the asteroid field. Some of the bigger asteroids look like we might be able to land and lie low while I fix the hyperdrive. We've got the parts, I just need a few hours to do the install."

That didn't sound terribly safe either, but Kerelle didn't have any better ideas.

"Well, that's half a plan then," she whispered. "Now let's go find Nalea."

Now that they were closer, Kerelle's awareness of Nalea had sharpened considerably. From what she picked up, their scientist was scared and bruised, but otherwise unharmed. She was also being held on a floor above them.

Trying not to think about how much further it would be to get back to the ship from the upper floor, she led them in what she hoped was the direction of the stairs. That hope proved incorrect, however, and they found themselves circling back through another corridor. The crowds of carousing pirates thinned considerably as they moved along, and Kerelle didn't have a great feeling about this corridor either. She supposed it would be too much to ask for one of those *you-are-here* maps like they had in shopping centers.

Abruptly she realized the corridor was empty except for herself, Sandrel, and a group of three pirates who'd been talking intently in low voices, and were now staring at them. Their eyes, narrowed in suspicion, were unfortunately clear - this group hadn't been hitting up the rum and ambrosia like the others they'd passed.

Kerelle upleveled their mental aura of anonymity, hoping the pirates' interest would vanish as she and Sandrel shuffled past with their buckets. Two of them responded as she'd hoped, their eyes sliding away. The third, unfortunately, was a bit sharper than his companions. And this was not a location he expected to see the cleaning staff.

"What are you doing in here?" he demanded sharply, leaning forward with a threatening air. That undid all of Kerelle's work with the other two, as they were reminded of her and Sandrel's presence. Their unfriendly stares now refocused on her.

"We're here to clean up," she answered, as guilelessly as she could. She lifted her bucket a little as if to show them, and zeroed in on the sharp one.

This was going to be tricky - press too hard, and they'd have a whole other set of problems. Gently but firmly, she tried to impress in his mind that there was something upstairs that was supposed to be cleaned. Upstairs was where the cleaners were supposed to go.

She sensed it starting to work. He couldn't think of what exactly, but the feeling that there was *something* these cleaners were supposed to be doing upstairs took root in his mind - accompanied by a heavy dose of irritation at the idiots they hire to keep this dump livable, who can't even get a simple task right. Kerelle seized on that, stoking his contempt for the compound's serving staff and using it to nudge him further. *Yes,* she urged, *the cleaners are too stupid to be upstairs where they belong. Make them go upstairs, so they can clean.*

"You're supposed to be cleaning *upstairs*, you lazy shits," he growled. "Up. Stairs. The stairs are *that way*. Take your slob buckets and move your asses before I tell the boss I caught you trying to slack off."

Thanks for the directions, sucker. Kerelle put her head down and mumbled something submissively as she turned the direction he'd indicated, Sandrel close on her heels. She let out her breath when they'd turned the corner.

"That was impressive," Sandrel murmured in her ear, "and impressively creepy."

"I'm just glad he went for it," she murmured back. "Hopefully any others we run into are either slower on the uptake or too spaced on ambrosia to notice we're here."

Luck was with them, and they found the stairs without further difficulty. They passed more pirates on the upper level, but as Kerelle had hoped, this lot was more concerned with partying than watching the cleaning staff. A few more hallways, and they were there.

"Nalea's in there," she whispered, indicating the large door at the other end of the hall with a bored-looking pirate standing guard. "Judging by its placement, and the extra security, I'm going to guess that's the brig."

"I'm going to guess you're correct," Sandrel answered. "I'm *also* going to guess they don't just wave in janitors who randomly show up to clean."

"Probably not," she agreed. "I think it's time to upgrade disguises."

They backtracked into the more populated section of the upstairs. Kerelle eyed the pirates they passed, finally selecting a loudly drunk pair who looked about the right sizes. She pushed on them both that there was something in the supply closet down the hallway they really wanted to see. They sprang up from against the wall at once to go investigate it.

The great thing about working with drunks was that one really didn't need to try that hard.

Six minutes and a pair of telekinetic blows to the back of the head later, Kerelle and Sandrel left the unconscious pirates bound and gagged in the closet and strode back down the hallway wearing their clothes. The fit was a bit loose on her purloined garb, but Kerelle thought she made a passable pirate. Sandrel made an *excellent* pirate, adopting a certain subtle swagger to his walk that helped sell it.

Thank the stars, Kerelle reflected, that she'd secured transport from someone great with disguises.

This time they walked right up to the door of the brig without hesitation, projecting the sense that they had every right to be there. The young pirate guarding the door looked them up and down with disinterest.

"You want something, then?"

"Boss said to check on the prisoner," Kerelle kept her voice low and rough, and hoped she was flattening her vowels enough to cover any Tallimau in her accent. Thank the stars she hadn't grown up there. She pushed on the guard not to notice - and not to ask for any clarification about the identity of "Boss."

She needn't have bothered. A quick mental read revealed the guard was bored, annoyed that she'd gotten stuck with prisoner duty, and had very little interest in excelling at her assignment.

"You lot can watch her then," the younger woman replied, tossing them a key card with a surly shrug. "I'm going for a drink." She waved at the brig door with annoyance and set off down the hall - possibly to ensure neither of them had time to argue.

Sandrel gave Kerelle a sidelong glance. "Was that you again?"

"Not this time." She angled the key card against the lock scanner. "Apparently it's hard to get good criminal help these days."

The door clanged shut behind them, and Kerelle's heart leapt. Nalea was huddled in the nearest cell.

Her eyes widened, and Kerelle hastily brought a finger to her lips. Nalea nodded jerkily and drew closer to the bars. Her wrists were bound and a large bruise had formed on one of her cheeks, but to Kerelle's great relief she looked otherwise unharmed.

"Are you alright?" She kept her voice in a low whisper as she knelt by the cell door.

"Alright enough to escape." Nalea held out her wrists; lacking a key, Kerelle simply blasted the cuffs apart. Fortunately for their continued stealth, the same keycard that opened the brig opened the cells.

Nalea massaged her wrists as Kerelle and Sandrel quickly filled her in. She was frightened, that much was clear even without the cold projections brushing against Kerelle's senses, but she only nodded grimly when they finished. "Let's get going then. I'll be happy to never see this place again."

The guard was still gone when they emerged, hopefully deep in a libation or three. They hustled along as fast as they dared, Nalea between them as if they were escorting the prisoner. It worked on the handful of pirates they passed on their way to the stairs; under Kerelle's mental urging they barely even looked up. *Escorting the prisoner. Routine business. Nothing worth noticing.*

It took a lot of attention to keep the telepathic shield up on all three of them, and Kerelle was so busy maintaining it she didn't sense the small knot of pirates around the corner until they had nearly walked into them. The group was walking in the opposite direction toward the brig, and looked significantly more alert than the ones down the hall. They all stopped, frozen in surprise.

Kerelle pushed hard with a stab of panic, trying to assert her narrative in their minds before they recovered. *We're escorting the prisoner to the boss. You* expect *this.*

They *didn't* expect it, though. In fact, they were on the way to collect the prisoner themselves, and so seeing her out of her cell with a pair of strangers was very much the opposite of what they expected. Kerelle pushed that there had been a change of plan, and for a wavering moment she thought it might work.

"Hey," one of them blurted suddenly, pointing at Sandrel, "That's Doylen's jacket. Who the fuck are *you*?"

Her mental hold on the group shattered like frozen glass.

TWENTY-THREE

THE PIRATES WHIPPED out their guns as Kerelle and Sandrel did the same, Kerelle trying to shove Nalea behind her. Even as she did so, she knew there were too many to fight, and no cover. Kerelle thought fast.

She pantomimed a quick throw and shoved them off their feet like marionettes. Hopefully they'd think she threw a concussion grenade, but there was no time to worry about it now. Kerelle grabbed Nalea's hand and broke into a run, Sandrel hot on her heels. The pirates' shouts of alarm echoed down the corridor behind them.

Well, noted the part of her mind prone to inappropriate levity, *this concludes the stealth portion of our escape.*

A shot hissed past her to scar the wall beside them - their assailants were back in pursuit. Kerelle threw up a telekinetic shield without a second thought, and the soft pops behind her confirmed it had been a good choice.

"Shield's up, don't fire behind us!" she yelled to Sandrel. "Focus on running, we have to get out." He gave her a tight nod and brought up his gun to aim ahead of them. Kerelle tried to follow her own advice and keep her eyes on the path ahead, trusting in her shield to guard their flank. By now the pirates behind them had to be noticing that their shots weren't connecting.

They could worry about repercussions if they survived this.

Rapid feet ahead of them, and another group of pirates burst into view. Sandrel didn't hesitate, and got off several shots before Kerelle shoved them all back hard against the wall. She kept the force up as they barrelled past. *These corridors are going to fill up fast.* Worse, she wasn't entirely sure where they were going. The fortress had been difficult to navigate *before* people were shooting at her.

Sandrel took a left at the fork without hesitation, and Kerelle decided to trust him. They sprinted down the corridor she hoped would bring them to the stairs.

Kerelle was aware that Nalea's breathing was growing labored, and that she was stumbling to keep up. She probably wasn't used to this kind of exercise, but they couldn't slow down. Kerelle kept a deathgrip on her hand and pulled the scientist forward as fast as she could.

It wasn't fast enough - the corridor behind them was a mass of pirates, rapidly catching up. Kerelle shoved them back into a heap, but the effort of holding the shield was highly distracting, and the psionic push didn't have as much force behind it as before. The pirates were soon up and closing again.

"Stairs!" Sandrel shouted, gesturing sharply. There they were up ahead - and already spilling over with pirates ready to head them off. Kerelle thought fast.

"Stay close and trust me!" she shouted back, and grabbed his hand to draw him over to her. Hopefully that trust was warranted, because this was either going to work brilliantly or kill them all. She was optimistic for the former. It wasn't that different in principle from what she'd done in the landslide on Elekar.

They closed on the stairs' landing, and she tightened the

shield into a shell around them. Rather than slowing down to engage pirates, she picked up speed, using her telekinetics to shove the shield along like a ball in an amusement game. The three of them were swept off their feet by the force of it, and Kerelle clutched Sandrel and Nalea tightly to her. *Closer, closer...*

The invisible sphere that shielded them rammed into the pirates at the mouth of the stairs, knocking them every which way, and kept going. Nalea screamed as they sailed over the side of the steps and free-fell down towards the ground floor.

Steady, steady, steady! Kerelle strengthened the shield beneath them with all she had, readying it to absorb the impact of the fall. It was a further distance than she remembered; if this didn't work the pirates would be scraping them off the tiles. Suddenly it wasn't far at all, and she clenched her teeth and *held.*

A teeth-clattering bounce, then another more gentle, and they rolled to an indifferent stop.

No time to recollect herself, or explore that painful twinge in her head that indicated she was starting to overdo it. Kerelle scrabbled to her feet and, bracing herself, ripped the chunk of stairs above them from the wall, flinging it up to crash into another stair segment so that they couldn't be followed. The twinge intensified. *Yep, definitely overdoing it.*

Sandrel was already on his feet as well, pulling up Nalea behind him. Nalea's ragged breathing had taken on a hysterical quality, but there was nothing to do but keep going. They ran.

It was cat and mouse after that, for what felt like years. Sandrel had done a better job than Kerelle of tracking their location in the base, and he led them back towards the hangar in fits of sprints and long pauses of hiding. The base was on full alert now, and the loudly relaxed bunches of revellers had been replaced by grim-faced groups with weapons at the ready.

They crouched around a corner as the latest group stalked past. The hangar was tantalizingly close now...and much more heavily guarded than it had been a few hours ago. Sandrel leaned over to whisper in her ear.

"We need to draw some off. If I toss a distraction, can you make them follow it?"

"I'll try. It'll be up to them if they take the bait, but I'll try to make it appealing."

"Hopefully you get enough to give us an opening. Even if we get to the ship in one piece, though, escape is going to be tight. Anything you can do to reduce their pursuit options will help."

She nodded slowly, remembering the small flock of ships they'd seen previously. The idea forming in her mind was probably more exertion than her tired psionics would appreciate, but none of it would matter if she met her end in a burst of pirate gunfire. Just another thing to toss on the rapidly growing pile of problems for later.

Sandrel gave her a nod and detached a compact device from his belt. He spun a few dials and arced it around the corner behind them.

The explosion wasn't powerful, but it was *loud*. Kerelle pushed on the pirates guarding the hangar that they needed to investigate the disturbance, it sounded like the fugitives. She wasn't sure if it was her influence or simple excitability, but the majority struck off to run down the other hall. Sandrel wasted no time, and dropped one of the remaining guards with a well-placed shot. Kerelle flung another against the wall with enough force to knock him unconscious while Sandrel dealt with the third. They sped inside.

The chaos of the hallways was multiplied in the hangar. Kerelle was forced to concentrate on shielding as they made a dash for the ship, Sandrel taking shots where he could manage them at the pursuers that seemed to flow from every direction. Kerelle grabbed his wrist and pulled him closer to her and Nalea as she sent a shockwave out around them, knocking over everyone in range. It gave them the precious seconds they needed to get to the ship.

"Hold them off!" Sandrel ordered as he leapt into the cockpit. Nalea sobbed quietly as she strapped herself in, her obvious terror strengthening Kerelle's resolve. It was Kerelle's fault Nalea was here at all, and by the stars Kerelle wouldn't let her die for it.

Ignoring her body's increasingly-unsubtle hints that she really ought to take it easy for a bit, Kerelle sent out another shockwave, knocking their pursuers back again. But it wasn't evading ground pursuit she had in mind - Sandrel was right, their opponents were already running for the small craft, no doubt intending to head them off from the air. About that.

She summoned her strength and grabbed the sleek fighter craft that looked like a military model - by far the biggest threat among the small craft. Nearby pirates shouted in alarm as it suddenly rose of its own accord. *Burning stars,* it was heavy. Kerelle gritted her teeth, adjusted her mental grip, and hurled it with all her might into the large viewport on the mothership's bridge.

The loud *crack* as the viewport glass gave way was extremely satisfying. The sight of the fighter stuck nose-first through the newly open-air viewport was even better.

"Nicely *done,* Fury," crackled over the intercom. "Might want to find a place to strap down." The engines thrummed beneath her feet.

Kerelle gave the seat beside Nalea a moment's wistful glance before sprinting for the gunnery.

She spun the guns around toward the remaining ships, getting a good shot in at the engines of a converted freighter. She was lining up for a second when the ship lurched and roared, and took off so quickly that only her harness saved her from being thrown against the viewport glass. Kerelle closed her eyes and clenched her jaw as her stomach protested its sudden, relentless upward trajectory. She forced her eyes back open to gauge how far the pirate ships were trailing them; not as close as she'd feared, but close enough she could get off a few shots behind them.

Sandrel's voice popped over the intercom again. "Get it out now, then all quiet once we hit atmosphere. We're almost through it."

Hoping he was right, Kerelle unloaded in a rain of fire behind them. The pirates were firing back now, and the shield alarms began to wail in protest. Sandrel pushed harder and she was thrown forward in her seat again. Her headache intensified, the pressure of their ascent compounding the strain of her earlier exertion.

Suddenly they hit the roar of atmosphere, and just as suddenly the silence of space. The rhythm of the engines had changed, she realized - the stealth field now hummed in the background.

"Everyone alright, I hope?" Sandrel's disembodied voice sounded tired. Kerelle could relate. "I'm taking us into the asteroid field for cover and to look for a landing spot. Stay belted just in case, but the hard part should be over."

It said something about how this day had gone, Kerelle thought, that "fly into an asteroid field and look for a landing spot" constituted the hard part being over.

TWENTY-FOUR

THE PAIN in her head brought her back to awareness, followed closely by a complaint from her shoulder. Kerelle groaned and blinked, her tired eyes feeling like they held an entire beach worth of grit. When her mind finally caught up with its surroundings, she discovered she'd fallen asleep still strapped into the gunnery chair. She shifted gingerly, her shoulder aching from the awkward angle she'd fallen asleep.

Maybe "passed out" was more appropriate.

Kerelle slumped back in the chair, indulging in a few moments of listless staring at the wall. Her head throbbed, all her muscles ached, and despite evidence to the contrary it felt like she hadn't slept in days. Getting up was not an appealing prospect.

She knew she *needed* to get up. She needed to check in on Nalea, and find out the ship's status from Sandrel, and see if either of them needed help she could provide. For once though, it was not the knowledge of unfulfilled responsibilities that finally rousted her - it was the knowledge that there was tea in the mess, and the only way to get some was to get up.

The ship was dark as she made her way slowly down the hall, with only the soft glow of the emergency lighting to guide her. Kerelle hoped that was related to repairs being in progress, and not indicative that she'd slept through a fresh catastrophe.

She turned the corner into the mess - and into suddenly much brighter light.

"You're up!" Nalea exclaimed. She was wrapped in a blanket, curled in the corner and clutching her own cup of tea. The portable light cube she'd absconded with from the base on Zharal V sat beside her. "And alive," she added somewhat belatedly. The addendum sounded more challenging than relieved, and her voice held the acerbic tone Kerelle was beginning to recognize as Nalea's response to stress.

"Was there a question about that?" Kerelle located the self-heating kettle half-hidden in shadow, and homed in like a guided missile. Tea wouldn't be enough to overcome the aftereffects of pushing herself too hard, but it would sure help get through them.

"After all that? I question how *any* of us are alive." She gave Kerelle a baleful look over her teacup. "If you'd gone and *died* after I put my whole life at risk to help you, I would have been really pissed. This is already a lot more than I signed up for."

"I know," Kerelle confessed. "I'm sorry this happened. I'm *especially* sorry you had to go through what you did."

"You and me both," the other woman muttered. The kettle dinged and Kerelle poured herself a cup as the silence stretched. After everything they'd just been through, she was very much not in the mood for this. She *really* just wanted to go back to her little cabin, drink her tea in peaceful solitude and then sleep until it didn't hurt to be awake.

She owed Nalea better than that.

With a moment's wistful thought of the empty cabin, she took a seat beside Nalea.

"What exactly happened, while we were gone?"

"There's not a lot to tell. You left to get parts, I stayed quiet like I was supposed to and kept everything locked. There was this huge bang, all the walls were shaking, and the next thing I know the door is open and there's a bunch of scary-looking people coming through. I tried to hide but not fast enough."

Kerelle paused, choosing her words carefully. "Did the pirates...hurt you at all?"

Nalea gave her another baleful look and gestured to her bruised face. "Well, they weren't exactly polite." She sighed and conceded the point. "They didn't torture me or anything, no. They didn't even really try to rough me up. The guy in charge yelled at me a lot and implied that getting roughed up was a possibility, something about learning respect for the Ash and Bones, but honestly? They weren't that interested in me."

She shrugged, though the overly casual gesture struck Kerelle as a cover for how upset she actually *was*. "I more or less told them the truth - I'm a passenger on this ship and I don't know what's going on. They seemed to believe it. Apparently I don't look like the daring pilot type."

Unsure whether she was supposed to agree or argue with that sentiment, Kerelle only nodded as Nalea continued.

"At that point they started talking about how much they might get for selling me, and then I started to freak out. I mean I *thought* you would probably come for me, since you need me to save your boyfriend, but I didn't *know*."

"I would have come for you regardless," Kerelle replied, a bit stung. Nalea looked unconvinced.

"So I told them who I was, and that Olstenfel would prob-ably pay ransom. At that point they just dumped me in the brig, and that's where I was until you and Sandrel showed up. No idea if they followed up on the ransom idea."

Kerelle digested that as she took a fortifying sip. "What would it mean if they did?"

Nalea's shoulders slumped a bit, the first crack in her porcupine defense mechanism that Kerelle had yet seen.

"I don't know," she finally answered. "It's a complication. It might actually help, or might make things even worse when this is over."

Kerelle opened her mouth to ask for clarification, and realized with an acute burst of shame that she'd never really *thought* about what this meant for Nalea afterwards, only about how she could get the help she needed. How very PsiCorp of her.

"What happens when this is over?" She felt her cheeks burn as she asked the question and hoped Nalea didn't notice. From the scientist's brittle smile, she noticed and was well aware of the cause.

"I go home, that's what happens. I call Olstenfel, tell them I escaped Zharal V in the chaos, ask for a ride home. They'll arrange something."

Kerelle gave her a startled glance. "Just like that? Is that... safe, after all this?"

Nalea shrugged again, though a touch of anxiety prickled at Kerelle's senses. "It's what an innocent woman would do."

"Besides," she continued with more confidence, "SysTech should have me down as disappearing in the same skirmish that supposedly killed you. There's no reason for them to suspect any shenanigans. Especially around committing an enormous crime and helping a high-level PsiCorp agent escape - it's not supposed to be possible, so it probably won't be the conclusion they jump to."

She laughed a little nervously then, as if the profundity of what she'd done was beginning to sink in. "But really SysTech has no reason to be interested in me. They'll probably just be thrilled they have one less prominent-scientist death for lawsuit fodder."

Nalea sighed heavily then and leaned back in her seat. Her earlier confidence faded. "But there *are* going to be questions," she admitted. "How I escaped Zharal on my own, and now about this whole pirate thing. And the longer I wait to check in, the bigger those questions are going to be. If I got kidnapped by pirates, that could explain why it took so long to get in touch, but then I have to explain how I *also* escaped from that..." she trailed off for a moment, staring into her now-empty cup.

Nalea's jaw hardened, and she met Kerelle's eyes with an almost defiant glare. "I'll think of something. Besides, even if the University suspects I'm not telling the whole story, I've got some insurance."

Kerelle raised her eyebrows. "Insurance?"

Nalea's lips curved into a mischievous half-smile. "I've got that whole shiny drive full of StellarEye data that nobody knows is missing. They'll be thrilled I have it, and they won't want to know where it came from."

Kerelle took a long sip of her tea, unable banish her concern. It was Nalea's life, and Kerelle had to trust her to make her own decisions, but she still thought the plan carried considerable risk. Still, she wasn't sure what help she might be able to offer - or, watching the stubborn set of her chin, what help Nalea might accept. Finally she just nodded and met Nalea's eyes.

"If you ever need help, I'm here for you. You don't have to do this alone."

"I'll keep that in mind," Nalea answered briskly, clear from her tone that she had no intention of doing so. The porcupine was once again in full force. "It's all pretty academic as long as this mission keeps dragging on. What's your game plan once we get off this rock?"

Kerelle drained her cup. "Get to the Morafer system, find Galhen, free him and escape."

Nalea stared at her. "I feel like that plan is missing a few steps."

"It needs some filling in once we get to Palhee," Kerelle acknowledged. "But since I have no idea where Galhen is in

Morafer, or what he's doing, or how to extract him from it, there's not much we can strategize around right now."

"So basically, you have no idea what we're going to do next. Glad to hear I upended my life for an airtight plan from the famous PsiCorp."

Kerelle bit back on an irritated response, aware that exhaustion was wearing on her patience. Nalea wasn't entirely wrong.

"Once we get to Morafer, we should be able to find more information on Senator Dalanva and her location," she explained. "When we get close enough I'll be able to contact Galhen telepathically and go from there."

Nalea was silent. Kerelle sighed.

"Once we find Galhen we'll need you to take his collar off as well," she conceded. "But after that, we can drop you off wherever you want. Galhen and I can find our own way after that."

"So." Nalea got up and crossed the room to refill her cup. "Guess we'd better get you close enough to call your boyfriend."

"Your brother," Kerelle corrected quietly.

Nalea's face tightened, and she looked away uncomfortably. She was silent as she kept her gaze on her teacup.

Kerelle sighed and got up. "Thank you for all your help so far. I'll go check with Sandrel on repairs, and I'll do my best to get you home as soon as possible."

Nalea didn't say anything as Kerelle headed out of the mess. It was probably too much to hope for that Sandrel would be in a better mood. And come to think of it, he *did* tell her he was throwing her off the ship at the first opportunity.

She sighed again, feeling bone-weary. One problem at a time.

―――――――――

KERELLE FOUND Sandrel in the engine room, half-hidden beneath an intricate mass of metal and wires. Screws and tools surrounded the smuggler as he lay on his back, humming softly as he deftly fastened something into place.

Well, that boded well for repairs.

She called out a greeting and he stopped humming, but didn't send her away.

"Can you pass me the arc skimmer?" He asked after a moment's silence. Kerelle's eyes darted around the tableau of scattered tools, looking for something that might be an arc skimmer. Her efforts were hampered by having no idea what an arc skimmer did.

"Um," she replied articulately, "is that the one with...."

Sandrel's easy laughter echoed from beneath the engine. "It's the one with the blue handle that says 'ArcTech' on the side, Fury."

Kerelle's cheeks warmed, but she couldn't help a smile as she deposited it in his outstretched hand. She had been expecting Sandrel to be as tense as Nalea - instead, this was the most relaxed she'd seen him.

She took a seat on the floor amidst the tools, and again he didn't send her away. Their adventure in the pirate base seemed to have put her back up a few notches in Sandrel's esteem. Being shot at together, she mused, did tend to be a bonding experience.

They stayed there a moment in companionable silence, broken only when Sandrel requested her assistance in passing him tools or holding engine bits. After all the stress and struggle of the last few days, it was almost pleasant to just sit quietly and listen. Sandrel, for his part, seemed content to fiddle with his engines.

"Will the ship be all right?" she asked finally.

"She'll be fine," he replied. "We took a lot of hits on the exterior, and I'll have to lay out a tall stack of credits to get her running perfect again, but the important things are all intact. Thrusters, life support..."

"The stealth field?" she asked teasingly.

"The stealth field," he agreed. His tone was amiable, but she detected a note of guard now. "Thank goodness, getting *that* fixed would be a mission in itself."

"Thank you for your help with everything." Even to her own ears it sounded woefully inadequate. "I'm sorry things got a bit more complicated than anticipated."

"Well, we got through it." His tone was decidedly noncommittal, and a marked contrast to his earlier easy warmth. The moment of camaraderie was over, and Kerelle tried not to miss it. She liked Sandrel, and she'd never been good at making friends.

Well, she couldn't blame him. She tried to keep the disappointment out of her voice. "So what will you do next?"

His hand paused mid-wrench. "Can't you just read my mind and find out?" The suspicion and discomfort was back in his voice. He might have forgotten what she was in the relief of the escape, but it was clearly back at the forefront of his mind. Just as clearly, it still bothered him.

Kerelle sat back on her heels and chose her words with care. "I *could*, yes. I have the ability, just like you have the ability to sabotage these engines or report me to the corporations or shoot me in my sleep. But just because I'm *able* to do something doesn't mean that I will. I can choose not to do it - and I hope you choose not to do any of those things either."

She couldn't see his face, and she didn't know if any of her words had landed. After a beat of silence he scooted out from under the engine apparatus to meet her eyes.

"So what's stopping you?"

"Well, I just told you I wouldn't, so if I do it anyway it would break my word and betray your trust. But even if I hadn't said otherwise, reading your mind without permission would violate your privacy, and I don't have a compelling reason to do that."

She realized she'd misstepped as his eyebrows lifted. "Oh, so as long as you have a *compelling reason* to rifle through my head without permission, then it's fine? Whatever *compelling* happens to mean?"

Backtracking would be akin to dishonesty, and compound the lies of omission that got them here in the first place. Kerelle lifted her chin and told him the truth.

"If our lives were in danger, and I thought I could save them by reading your thoughts? Then yes, I'd do it. If I just want to know what you're thinking? That's not good enough."

She sighed. "Sometimes I can pick up on what you're feeling, because you're feeling it strongly enough that it broadcasts. We call that *projecting*. Telepaths can intentionally project thoughts and feelings to others. It's how we're able to communicate mind-to-mind. But mundanes still unconsciously project strong thoughts and emotions to people around them. I keep low-level psychic shields up all the time to block out projections from people around me - otherwise I'd go mad - but sometimes especially strong projections get through."

Kerelle paused as Sandrel remained silent. She could stop here and hope he was mollified, possibly enough so to help with the next stage of the mission. It was most of the truth anyway.

No.

It was most of the truth...and more lies-by-omission. Sandrel deserved better from her, and she wanted to *be* better. The shame at realizing how little she'd considered Nalea's risk still settled around her like a stifling coat. She couldn't blame SysTech any more - she was making her own choices, and they needed to be better choices than SysTech would make.

"Sandrel, the truth is, I *did* read your mind, the very first time we met in the bar on Zharal V and I was terrified you would recognize what I was and sell me out to SysTech. It was wrong, and I *knew* it was wrong, and I did it anyway. I'm sorry."

Outrage lit his eyes and he sat all the way up. "I remember I didn't want to take the job, and you convinced me anyway. Did you *convince* me?" His emphasis on the word was almost a sneer.

"*No*," she told him emphatically. "I read your mind quickly and saw that you weren't thinking of betraying me, and then I backed off. All the *convincing* was entirely mundane - I upped the payment to sweeten the deal, just like anyone else would."

More softly, she added, "I really am sorry, Sandrel. It was wrong and all I can do now is apologize. That was the only time, and it won't happen again."

He said nothing, his face completely closed. He didn't look at her.

It was Kerelle who finally broke the silence again.

"Case in point, right now I would really *like* to know what you're thinking. But I'm not going to look. I have to ask instead."

His eyes cut up to hers. "You realize I only have your word that you *aren't* looking."

"Sandrel, I can't change what I am. I can't change what I've done. All I can do is tell you the truth and hope that you accept it. I spent my whole life being forced to do whatever the company wanted, whether it was right or wrong. I don't know that I'll ever be able to make up for what I did for them, but I can't change the past. All I can do now is try to do right instead of wrong." *And we're off to a* great *start on that,* she thought bitterly. But what she said to Sandrel was true - there was only forward.

He was quiet for a moment.

"You know the crazy part," he finally said softly, "is that I kind of believe you." He picked up the arc skimmer and inspected it, not looking at her as he continued. "I still feel like you're way more trouble than I signed up for, but I guess I already signed up, didn't I?"

He dropped the arc skimmer into the tool box and met her eyes. "So, mind telling me what I *did* sign up for?"

She told him everything. Growing up at the PsiCorp base on Hasha. Transferring to Tallimau in her early teens for advanced multi-gift training, and meeting Galhen there. How they'd stayed together for the intervening decade, despite frequent separation and the rigors of their respective roles. How those roles had seemed increasingly untenable, and the indoctrination of their upbringing began to lose its hold. Elekar. Senator Dalanva. The escape on Zharal V.

At some point they moved to the mess, and they both had whiskey by the time she finished. Sandrel was quiet throughout the story, simply listening to her talk, and she was surprised by how good it felt to talk about it. She felt utterly wrung out at the end, but in a good way - as though she'd drained a festering wound.

They were both quiet for a moment. Sandrel downed the rest of his whiskey.

"Morafer's a big place, and I'd rather not fly around blind. I guess once we get to Palhee, we need to figure out where your boyfriend is at." His tone was diffident, as if this had always been the plan - as if what he just said hadn't carried an enormity in its words.

Kerelle's throat went tight and her eyes began to sting, but she managed to thank him anyway without dissolving into an awkward mess. From his small smile, he was well aware that she was near tears, but he only nodded and went back to check on the engines.

Kerelle made it back to her cabin before the sobs escaped, and then she couldn't hold them in. Everything that had happened over the last few weeks caught up with her at last, and she finally fell apart, gasping for breath as her thin pillow soaked through with tears. But the breakdown felt more cathartic than detrimental, and as she stared up at the ceiling all she could think of was that *they had done it,* after all.

She'd escaped the collar. She'd escaped SysTech, she'd

escaped Zharal V, she'd escaped Kalnis. They'd done it, and now there was nothing in the way of finding Galhen. She would free him too, they would escape Dalanva, and then finally perhaps those dreams wouldn't seem so far-fetched after all.

I'm coming, love. And soon nothing will be the same.

THANK YOU FOR READING!

I'm so glad you came along with Kerelle on her adventures. Of course, she still has a lot left to do - for one thing, she still doesn't have a firm plan for rescuing Galhen…

Read on for a sneak peek at what comes next, and if you liked this book, **please consider leaving a review on Amazon or Goodreads**. It really does help indie books find the people who want to read them!

THE STORY CONTINUES IN THE STARS UNBOUND

Kerelle Evandra has done the impossible: she's broken free of her control collar and escaped the PsiCorp. For the first time in her life, her fate is in her own hands. But Kerelle didn't escape for only her own sake. Her lover Galhen is still being held at a powerful oligarch's estate, and she didn't come this far just to abandon him now.

Kerelle and her allies devise a daring plan to rescue Galhen - but success comes at a terrible price, and they are left trying to find a way forward in a future they never imagined. Kerelle and Galhen soon discover that a new life outside SysTech holds its own set of questions, and they're running out of time to find the answers.

They may be looking toward the future, but as old threats resurface, it's clear that the past - and the PsiCorp - isn't done with them yet.

Keep reading for a preview of **The Stars Unbound** (Gift of the Stars, Book 2), available now on Amazon!

THE STARS UNBOUND: CHAPTER 1

Palhee, Kerelle mused as she munched her snack, was easily the second-seediest place she had ever been - and if they'd made it here without the detour to Kalnis, it would assuredly top the list. The streets were narrow and winding, snaking haphazardly between shabby shops and crowded apartments, and seemed perpetually dim. Those same narrow streets were lined by vendors hawking all manner of wares, ranging from probably-not to quite-obviously stolen. Of those people packing said streets, many had the air of those who tried to avoid attention.

But at the same time, Palhee was nothing like Kalnis. The site of their ill-fated repair stop had been a psychic mire of misery and despair. There was misery and despair here as well, of course, but there was also hope and excitement and opportunity. Adventures were planned over spiced coffee, in shops tucked away between larger businesses. Children played in the packed blocks' nooks and crannies. Interspersed within the merchant stalls were food vendors, and a faint, delicious aroma wafted above the open-air market.

It was fascinating.

Sandrel had planted her at the edge of the market, procured

her something to eat and instructed her to wait for his return. While she felt a bit like a child being kept out of trouble while her parents were busy, Kerelle really didn't mind much. It gave her an excellent opportunity to simply sit back and observe the world around her - a world that, for the first time in her life, was not reacting to her as a PsiCorp agent. Simply being ignored as part of the throng was a new experience in itself.

Whatever it was she was eating was rather excellent as well. It was some sort of fruit pastry, fried, rolled in sugar, and served on a stick. Nalea had earlier declined to leave the sanctuary of the ship, but Kerelle thought these pastries might be able to lure her out. The only reason Kerelle herself wasn't eating a second one was because she lacked the hard currency to buy it.

She was idly contemplating how many pastries one of her earrings might be worth when Sandrel rematerialized out of the crowd.

"You're still here," he observed with note of teasing. "I think that means this is the longest we've gone without a disaster since I met you."

She raised her now-sadly-empty pastry stick in a salute. "Glad you noticed. I've been trying to improve." She cocked an eyebrow. "I take it your business was successful?"

"That it was. Got us a price I can live with, we bring the ship in tomorrow. Should take about a week to get everything back up to top shape."

"Was there doubt about the price? I thought you and the owner were friends?"

"We are. That's why he's only charging me an arm and a leg instead of two, especially for one week turnaround on that kind of damage." Sandrel shrugged, a half smile on his lips "Really, he's just being generous. Gerunel runs the best repair yard on Palhee. I can pretend to haggle, but we both know I wouldn't trust my baby with anyone else here."

Kerelle couldn't resist. "Particularly since your baby has

some non-standard modifications?"

Sandrel threw back his head and laughed. "This is *Palhee*, Fury. If I didn't have some kind of *non-standard modifications* they'd assume I was an undercover marshal."

Kerelle smiled back, a warmth spreading in her chest. Things had been different between her and Sandrel since their talk in the engine room. Their pilot treated her less like a bothersome client and more like, well, an actual friend. He'd even offered to give her a hand going incognito - which was the very reason she was waiting here now.

Sandrel offered her his grip and pulled her up from her seat. "So, you ready to get started?"

She nodded her affirmative and they set out through the throng of people, Kerelle taking care to stick close. She could find Sandrel telepathically if she lost him, of course, but she'd prefer not to get lost at all.

"So I'm thinking our first stop is to get you some currency in a more practical increment than 'small fortune,'" he murmured in her ear as they passed through the next block. "That jewel collection of yours was a clever idea, but it's not exactly practical now that you've actually made it out."

Kerelle nodded her emphatic agreement. "The only reason I didn't have more of those pastries you bought me is that I didn't think the stall vendor could make change for platinum."

He gave her a surprised grin. "You liked the *ranla*, then?"

"Is that what it's called? It was delicious."

"Glad you think so. They were my favorite thing when we lived on the Station, you don't find a lot of people that make them planetside. Palhee's one of the only places with enough station brats to make a market."

"You're a station kid?" It made sense; many spacer families either lived in their ships or on one of the artificial port stations dotting the galaxy. And many space-born people followed in their parents' footsteps and became spacers themselves.

"Sort of. We just lived on the ship when we were hauling freight, but there were few years we lived part-time on a station in the Olnarr Ring," he answered. "Didn't really appreciate it until I got older. When I was a kid it seemed like planetside always had a better version of everything. Then I started taking my own jobs and actually spending time on solid ground. It's overrated."

She sorted through that. "Was your ship your parents' ship, first?" She'd heard that some ships were passed down through generations of spacer families, a home and a livelihood all in one.

"Nah, I bought her with a lot of hard-earned money. Mom sold theirs after Dad died."

He stopped and waved her towards a nondescript door. "And here we are. Let me do the talking."

Even if they hadn't arrived when they did, Kerelle sensed Sandrel didn't care to say anything else on the subject. She gave a mental shrug and followed him through the door. It was none of her business anyway.

The pawn shop was barely more than a closet; Kerelle could nearly touch both walls of cluttered, overflowing shelves from the center of the room. Kerelle eyed the haphazard stacks of dusty junk with a skepticism she tried to keep off her face. This certainly wasn't anywhere she would have stopped, but she trusted Sandrel to know what he was doing.

The owner looked as ancient and run-down as his goods. He peered over the counter at them with a combination of disdain and suspicion.

Sandrel greeted him loudly in a dialect Kerelle couldn't quite follow. The old man groused back in the same dialect, but his shoulders seemed to relax a bit. After some back and forth Sandrel leaned over to whisper in her ear. "Just the two pendants and the earrings we set aside earlier. We'll unload the rest elsewhere."

Even with just a portion of her collection, Kerelle walked away with an impressive stack of credits. Sandrel thanked the old man enthusiastically in words she couldn't understand, receiving a disinterested grunt in return. He waved and steered her out of the shop.

"So did that go...well?" she asked curiously.

"It went great. Olen was thrilled, he'll be able to sell those at a huge markup. Plus he usually gives you a break in commission if you chat him up in Starna."

Kerelle was learning all kinds of things today. "Starna?"

"It's a dialect from the stations in the Olnarr ring. I picked it up when we lived there." He cocked his head at her. "You didn't go slumming much, did you?"

Kerelle gave him a rueful laugh. "The Olnarr Ring is definitely not a vacation spot that would make it through management approval."

The scene repeated itself throughout the afternoon, as Sandrel led her to a series of out-of-the-way establishments. Most of the proprietors spoke Standard, though a few carried on lively conversation in Starna. By the end, she'd traded away nearly all her jewelry, and in return she'd acquired what even she could recognize was an eyebrow-raising amount of credits. Even after divvying up what she owed Sandrel for the escape from Zharal V - which was an eyebrow-raising amount in itself - she still found herself a wealthy escapee.

Sandrel seemed impressed in spite of himself. "They *did* pay you well, didn't they?"

"They didn't pay me at all," she reminded him. "That's why I stuffed everything of value in my pockets on the way out."

"Well, that will make this next part easier," Sandrel observed cheerfully. "It's time to be someone else."

Kerelle couldn't stop staring at her hair. It didn't really *look* like "her" hair anymore - that was the point, after all, but she was still fascinated. It was shorter than it had ever been, the longest tips barely brushing her shoulders, with added layers cut shorter still to frame her chin. She was surprised what a difference it made.

Initially she'd thought she should dye it, but Sandrel had said no - her only option was to go lighter, and that would look attention-grabbingly artificial. Instead, he'd half-dragged her into a fashionable salon.

"Don't change your hair, change how you wear it. Agent Evandra is a practical sort who doesn't bother with how she looks," he'd told her bluntly. "Disguise yourself as someone who does."

As counter-intuitive as it had seemed to make herself less noticeable with a trendy haircut, she trusted Sandrel's judgement when it came to lying low. Now that she'd done it, she could see what he meant. The woman staring back at her looked like any number of others she'd passed by on Palhee. She certainly *didn't* look like Senior Agent Kerelle Evandra's file photo.

Besides, the ID in her pocket said Karia Vela Vendrys now. Apparently Karia went to nice salons.

After more staring, and a few experimental shakes of her head to watch the midnight strands move, Kerelle decided she liked the new look. Hopefully Galhen liked it too.

She also hoped he liked the clothes she'd bought him. It was only a few pieces, acquired alongside her own new wardrobe, but it had felt good to pick them out - a statement of intent that she was actually going to rescue him. That his presence would be real, and not just a constant hovering memory.

And for that to happen, she needed to get to work.

The first step to rescuing Galhen was figuring out where he was. The first step to doing *that* was figuring out where the senator was.

A datanet search on Senator Dalanva turned up a surprising amount of information, which could be generally divided into two types: dry parliamentary records, and the society pages. It was the second one that grabbed her attention.

Estia Parie Dalanva was clearly a fixture in Morafer high society. There was a regular cadence of mentions in connection with charity balls, genteel sporting events, and so on, as well as parties hosted in multiple estates on multiple planets. There was also, however, a flurry of coverage of Dalanva's recent acquisition of a Class 3 psionic aide, the first time such a valuable asset had been leased to a private individual. It had, apparently, been something of a social coup.

Some of the society papers were admiring, others professed to be scandalized by what must have been an astronomical expense. None were even slightly interested in how Galhen might be a human being with his own feelings about all this, and referred to him like some sort of prizewinning horse. Kerelle's jaw hurt from clenching by the time she finished the stack.

She also didn't know much more than when she started, except that this Dalanva woman and the whole Morafer system could go straight to the burning void. She supposed if worst came to worst, they could start crashing benefit galas and trust they'd run into her eventually.

With a sigh she turned her attention to the parliamentary records. She wasn't optimistic that Dalanva's voting record on transportation spending was going to be enlightening, but -

Oh stars and blood. She should have come here first.

The news story covered some speech Dalanva had recently given on the Senate floor, with an embedded clip of video. The senator was an elegant older woman and a charismatic speaker, but Kerelle tuned her out to stare at the entourage standing a few paces behind her. Closest to the Senator's left was Galhen.

Kerelle stopped the video and simply stared, her pulse racing. It was really him.

He'd cut his hair too - it was shorter now and neatly slicked back, not a style she'd seen on him before. It was well matched with the military-inspired uniform he wore, cut to emphasize both his lean build and the collar. Prominent on the jacket was an intricate design Kerelle recognized from the society papers as Dalanva's personal crest.

Overall the effect was impeccable. Standing behind Dalanva, posture perfect and face impassive, he looked like something out of a fashion feature. Cold but beautiful, dangerous but contained.

He did not look at all like the warm and loving partner she'd known half her life.

Dalanva finished her speech and descended the dais to thunderous applause. Smoothly Galhen offered her his arm, and she took it as they headed out of the senate chamber, assistants following in a tight knot. The camera cut closer to Dalanva - close enough she could see Galhen better as well. His face was set in a serene mask, but there was a terrible emptiness in his eyes.

She watched it three more times.

The door of their rented suite opened to admit Sandrel and Nalea, both carrying full armloads of whatever they'd gone to the market for.

"You missed it, Fury," Sandrel called. "There was a line around the block for these dumplings and this guy-" he cut off as he saw her face. "Kerelle, what happened?"

She waved them both over and played the video again. Nalea watched silently, expression inscrutable as she saw her brother for the first time in twenty-five years. Sandrel glanced between the two of them, then back to the video.

"That's your man, isn't it."

Kerelle just nodded. Sandrel was quiet as they watched the rest. When it was over, he looked over at her.

"So I know this is the whole reason we're here," Sandrel said carefully. "But he doesn't seem to be... in distress... exactly. And Dalanva seems to keep her people comfortable. I know you saw those records, but they could have been an error. Are you sure he's going to want to leave to come be an intergalactic fugitive?" His voice was neutral, but the unspoken question was deafening. He was asking if they were staging a kidnapping.

"I'm sure." She knew she sounded defensive but she couldn't help it. "He looked unhappy. I know him well enough to see it."

She was aware of how weak that argument sounded, even without his response.

"That's what you *want* to see," he told her gently. "But are you sure it's what *he* wants?"

She wanted to snap back that of *course* it was, but Kerelle forced herself to take a deep breath and disengage her storming emotions. She understood his point, even if she didn't like it.

"We know where they are now," she said. "We can head to the area. When we get close enough, I'll be able to contact Galhen with my powers. If he says..." she had to force it out. "If he says he wants to stay, then that will be the end of it."

She stood up then and headed for her temporary room. "It's been a long day. I think I'm going to lie down."

Sandrel watched her go with concern, but he said nothing, and neither did Nalea, who seemed lost in her own thoughts. Kerelle shut the door behind her and slumped down against it, feeling sick at heart.

Galhen would want to leave with her. She knew he would.

What if he didn't?

The Stars Unbound is available on Amazon!

ABOUT THE AUTHOR

Lena Alison Knight grew up reading space opera and high fantasy, and started writing her own as soon as she could hold a crayon steady. She lives with her husband in the San Francisco Bay Area, and when not writing she can be found taking brisk walks, haunting local coffee shops, or sprawled on the couch playing video games.

You can find her online at lenaalisonknight.com, and join her newsletter to keep up with what's coming next.

Made in United States
Orlando, FL
28 July 2022

20248302R10140